THE WOODEN SWORDS

THE WOODEN SWORDS

NEIL L. MARCHESE

PALMETTO
PUBLISHING
Charleston, SC
www.PalmettoPublishing.com

The Wooden Swords
Copyright © 2023 by Neil L. Marchese

Paperback ISBN: 979-8-8229-3400-9

CONTENTS

PROLOGUE

Buddy had vivid recollections of the Blue Ridge Vista property because a buyer offered the full asking price: $35 million for the 850-acre tract of land. More important to Buddy was the $700,000-plus commission he would pocket, the largest ever in his real estate career. There was just one issue that Buddy hadn't resolved with the listing agent prior to the sale. Buddy had verbally agreed to a cobroker position on the property. He had done a tremendous amount of the work, and $700,000 was a lot of money. But he didn't mind the work at all, and he loved the Blue Ridge Vista property. Besides, the broker was his friend— at least he thought so. It was a model senior living facility that was serene and breathtakingly beautiful. No expense had been spared to build the incredible complex.

Buddy should have known better, but this cobroker arrangement had worked well for him in the past, and besides, Buddy was not much for details; he just wanted to sell, and that was his problem. Buddy would soon learn that the listing broker had no plans to share the commission with him.

The land deal had taken months to execute. There were three different sellers, two of whom were out of state, and property deeds and title searches to review, as the property's ownership dated back to the 1700s. The EverStar Group had engaged the Kaufman Law Firm, who traced the property origins of the Blue Ridge Vista location in their due diligence process. T. Randall Kaufman II also knew the historical significance of the 250-acre tract on the southeast portion of the larger property, which would make any plans for development next to impossible. While he wasn't sure who the owners were, he did know Virginia law well enough to know that EverStar would have a battle to complete their project. But just to secure the EverStar Group's influence in any future litigation, they advanced the Kaufman Law Firm a $5 million retainer to cover any interference they might encounter. This advance by EverStar was also the reason for T. Randall's exodus from the firm. The senior partners voted him out in a lopsided coup.

There were environmental impact studies and state and county regulatory agencies to deal with, as well as utility easements—all of which made for an exhausting and time-consuming ordeal. Combined with COVID-19, it was remarkable that the deal was completed at all. The restrictions placed on businesses trying to finish their work before the sale created hurdles at every phase of the transaction.

The day before the closing, a private equity group out of Boston offered 25 percent more, which made Buddy's pain even greater. Not only did Buddy lose out on the first attempted purchase, but he also took a double shot to the gut when the entire transaction was completed.

The second buyer guaranteed to close in thirty days, no contingencies. As with many land development projects, the first buyer overpays and by a lot. In this case, it didn't matter because in an instant, Buddy's dream and hard work vanished. He was ruined. There was speculation of a behind-the-scenes political twist involving some cabinet members and high-ranking congressmen, but there wouldn't be any investigation—that is, not until some four years later.

Buddy not only lost the cobroker fee on the sale of the Blue Ridge Vista deal, but his wife had been funneling his agency real estate profits to a villa in Saint Thomas. Her vision and planning did not include Buddy.

Margo and Buddy's cobroker commission vanished. He would file for bankruptcy and eventually land a sales gig at Blue Ridge Vista. The only salvation was that Buddy would get a patio home to live in as part of his compensation. There was a catch—his home would be used as a model for prospective residents, so he had to keep it clean all the time. It was better than any option he had, and he knew it.

Blue Ridge Vista was the premier senior living community in the state of Virginia. The original owners had secured the big names in professional sports, medicine, politics, and media to do countless promos for the facility in the early stage of development. Their advertising budget was in the millions. Blue Ridge Vista promoted itself as a high-end enterprise, focused on the special amenities: chefs, florists, health salons, entertainment, special transportation, and other elegant touches. There would be no expense spared for the residents; their families would rest easy knowing their loved ones lived at Blue Ridge Vista. The luxury accommodations included private suites in the main facility and beautiful two- and three-bedroom villas with spectacular views of the majestic and gently rolling hills of central Virginia. Serenity was for sale, for the right price. The Blue Ridge Vista plans also included an architectural rendering of the phase two expansion with another twenty-five villas; the site work and infrastructure were already under construction.

Blue Ridge Vista had a calligrapher on staff who was part of Buddy's closing technique. Imagine a table set on the veranda of Blue Ridge Vista, name cards positioned for each family member, and a stunning view of the grounds. Buddy had the stage set. There would be coffee, tea, and water with lemon in crystal glasses. The appointments were always at 10:00 a.m., and Buddy was always ten minutes late. He waited off to the side with his cell phone to his ear, pretending to listen, only watching the soon-to-be residents admiring the beauty of Blue Ridge Vista. At precisely 10:10, Buddy would casually walk to the table, his phone to his ear, still listening to no one. Buddy would apologize quietly to the guests at the table and motion with his hands just enough for them to hear him say, "Thank you so much. I know you will be happy with your decision."

Buddy was about six feet tall, very handsome, with grayish wavy hair that was a bit long but not too long. He dressed to the nines: linen khaki slacks, Armani loafers, no socks, light-blue pinstripe shirt, and blue tailored jacket. This was his uniform on game day, and today was game day.

"I apologize for being late. I was fortunate to have another family join our family here at Blue Ridge Vista. They just purchased a two-bedroom villa on Willow Court, not far from my home.

"Have you ever seen such a beautiful and calming view, ever? I know I haven't. This is what your mother will enjoy in the mornings, afternoons, or evenings as often as she would like. It's the most tranquil setting I have ever seen."

Buddy was staring and waiting for the next question, which usually took less than two minutes.

"Excuse me, Buddy, could you tell us how many villas are still available? I mean, if you could."

Buddy was a Picasso with a different canvas. He was enjoying his painting.

Buddy would be the guy to cash flow the operation by selling the villas before they were built. A 50 percent down payment was required to secure a Blue Ridge Vista residence. Buddy was well compensated for his effort with a villa of his own, under the condition that it would be used as a model for future residents' viewing. He didn't mind because he needed the money.

What Buddy hadn't planned on was COVID-19 and the financial mismanagement of Blue Ridge Vista. A series of Medicare issues and state licensing problems drew Blue Ridge Vista into a death spiral.

The almost $2 million in deposits that Buddy had secured were gone along with the two top executives. Buddy had been had once again. A court-appointed guardian to oversee the transition was put in place by a federal judge because of the Medicare fraud. The guardian's charge was to find a buyer, and with some bridge financing, in less than thirty days EverStar seized the opportunity to help. This kind of help was purchased for pennies on the dollar, as EverStar was not going to miss this chance to acquire the 850 acres and Blue Ridge Vista a second time. A former EverStar executive who was a competitor was responsible for closing the initial sale of the property and the Blue Ridge Vista Senior Care Facility.

EverStar came to the rescue, and they expedited the closing knowing the complete history of the property. The judge agreed to the EverStar offer, much to the displeasure of many creditors. EverStar had much bigger plans: create two LLCs—one for the Blue Ridge Vista Senior Care Facility and the other for the land and their planned new gated community with a championship golf course. EverStar's internal financial analysts projected the land, the homes, and the golf course to be worth in excess of $1 billion.

The Knights—T. Randall Kaufman II, Robert Stewart, Ben Schein, and Salvatore Romano—would be new residents at Blue Ridge Vista. An attorney, a real estate executive, a jeweler, and a carpenter, all retired and all looking forward to their new and beautiful surroundings. The Knights were an unlikely crew of personalities who shared a common love for their new home and each other.

Chapter One:

THE KNIGHTS

T. Randall Kaufman II was a senior law partner specializing in corporate law and real estate. He was the son of the founder of the most influential Washington, DC, law firm, which was formed in 1939. T. Randall's father was thirty years old when he started the law practice.

T. Randall Sr. 's inauspicious start in the DC real estate scene was doing a favor for a first-year senator from New York. The senator was looking for a home in the Bethesda area, and T. Randall reviewed the deed and contract for sale within one day and comped his fee as a gesture of trust that the senator might refer other colleagues. That "favor" proved to be transformational for his newly created law practice.

The Kaufman Law Firm was well on its way to gaining the prominence that would have taken years to establish in 1939. Within a year, the Kaufman Law Firm grew to eight associates. Two additional partners would solidify the Kaufman, Rogers, and Daniels Law Firm as the preeminent DC legal practice.

It was only natural, based on their clients' needs and the firm's influence, to expand into corporate law.

T. Randall's Rolodex was the pathway to the firm's future. The firm was always able to facilitate a client request with a phone call within their guarded network of DC influencers.

In 1945, Kaufman, Rogers, and Daniels had grown to twenty-five employees: six attorneys on the real estate side, nine specializing in corporate law, five paralegals, one receptionist, and four secretaries.

As DC's suburbs grew in the 1950s and 1960s, so did the clout of the practice. The growth of the Kaufman Law Firm helped move their practice to a prominent location two blocks from the nation's capital It only made sense, as did the rise in their professional fees, which were never an issue for any of their clients.

T. Randall was like his father in many ways: they were both Harvard undergraduates and Harvard Law School honors graduates. Like many children who benefit from the labor of their fathers, T. Randall was an exemplary professional. He absolutely loved the practice of law. His talent and hard work helped him develop phenomenal negotiating skills that, combined with a detail-driven personality, made him the firm's most prized asset.

T. Randall now guided the real estate side of the firm's practice, and there was never a member of the group who questioned his talent or work ethic. He immersed himself in local and jurisdictional disputes in Maryland and Virginia. His real estate focus would later prove to be consequential for one of the nation's largest and most influential private equity companies.

He married his college dream girl and moved into a stately Bethesda home, where they raised three children. Randall's wife loved the lifestyle made possible by his sixty-hour work weeks, excluding weekends. His wife and children wanted for nothing throughout their lives. As the children grew, so did the lavish taste and expectations of travel and experience, both domestically and internationally. Unfortunately for T. Randall, many of the excursions did not include him.

T. Randall's work and vision helped expand the firm to an office of fifty, with annual billings north of $50 million. The Kaufman Law Firm was not DC's largest, but it was by far the most prominent and influential. The year was 2000, and things were in a good place for the firm, but his life and purpose were going to change in a way he couldn't imagine.

Robert William Stewart, or Buddy, was "the guy." He never met a stranger, and he lit up a room like a Fourth of July celebration. He could talk the bark off a tree. He was a professional bullshitter but a good guy.

Buddy's career path was the opposite of T. Randall's. Hard work was an aberration; enjoying life and being with friends was his course of collegiate direction. Buddy graduated from an excellent university able to dodge his most despised academic requirement: a foreign language. Buddy had a plan, as he would explain on occasion.

"I'm going to wait and see if they'll change their mind on the foreign language thing," he would say. That was his plan. Before his senior year, his plan came together as the foreign language requirement was removed from the curriculum. Buddy's new tagline, "No hablo Española," was beneath his senior composite picture in 1970.

Buddy's low-stress demeanor was disarming to the serious and more highly focused members of the Beta Iota fraternity. On more than one occasion, freshmen would marvel at Buddy's casual approach to the rigors of academic life. When asked by an underclassman how he could party like he did and study,

Buddy would reply with something like "You just got to establish your priorities," or "It's not as easy as I make it look," or "It's a secret. Just kidding. I struggle sometimes, but I have found that practice makes perfect."

Each response would elicit a facial expression of bewilderment.

During fraternity rush, Buddy would ice down a case of beer, try to clean his room, turn up ZZ Top on his stereo, and maybe fire up a blunt (only to relax himself). He'd even take a shower. Truth be known, preparing for fraternity rush was the hardest Buddy ever worked. Other upperclassmen dreaded the whole rush thing, but Buddy loved it. He was like the captain of a football team pacing in the living room with a pep talk. The other guys in the fraternity stared at him, stunned, while he pretended to be Vince Lombardi.

At graduation, Buddy's best friend waited for him to walk off the dais, both raising their faux diplomas.

"Buddy, I can't believe it; we got out of here!" he said. "I can't believe we got in," Buddy responded.

After graduating with a degree in sociology, Buddy wandered from sales job to sales job, finally settling into a career in real estate, achieving numerous sales awards—the Round Table, for sales in excess of $2 million, and the President's Club, for three consecutive years of million-dollar sales, were special accomplishments. In a relatively short time, Buddy became the guy you wanted to list your property or business with. He had established a phenomenal network of contacts and clients in a somewhat brief career.

Within two years of starting in real estate, he opened his own office. Because Buddy was not into the details of finance and operating a business, his wife, Margo, a successful agent herself, would be the one to manage the day-to-day operations within the business The real estate market was booming in the late 1990s and early 2000s, and Buddy and Margo were on a glide path and living large, or at least Buddy thought so.

On occasion, Buddy's group would work with the Kaufman firm on transactions for important and well-connected members of the elite DC crowd. The growth and good fortune for both enterprises proved profitable and exciting. The prominence was not unnoticed by the print and social media; Facebook created an entirely new network to promote their work and success—until 2015.

A brutal divorce from Margo left Buddy financially ruined. His wife had filtered the real estate profits to an offshore Bahamas account, where she and her new lover had stashed over $3 million. Buddy had little time left to try to regain some type of financial footing. He was able to close the sale of over twenty-five units in the senior living community. Things could be worse; Buddy was seventy-four and still selling.

Benton Gustav Schein Jr.—Ben—was the only son of Romanian Jews who were able to flee Europe in 1945. The Scheins' trek through other European cities convinced them that America was the hope they longed for, like many others who sought to escape persecution.

Benton Sr. and Erma arrived in New York and would eventually settle in a small city in Indiana. Ben's father had worked for a jeweler as a precious stone grader and goldsmith, acquiring unique skills as a fine craftsman. Ben would work in his family's store in every aspect of the jewelry business, preferring tasks for which he could use the fine motor skills he developed in stone setting and design. The family lived in a three-bedroom flat above the Schein Jewelry and Watch Repair Shop, a half block off Main Street.

Having lived through the Depression, the Scheins understood the value of a simple and frugal lifestyle. Their discipline propelled their business in Indiana as Erma would greet the customers and keep the books, while Ben Sr. was able to expand their precious stones collection. His ability to create special ring and bracelet settings and to repair watches minimized the business expense of using a third party for the same services. The Schein family business enjoyed a comfortable growth while young Ben honed his skills under the tutelage of his father and mother. His hunger to learn and master the jewelry trade did not leave much time for young Ben to interact with other children outside of the normal school year. The time he spent with others his age was uncomfortable and awkward.

While in grade school and middle school, Ben gained some confidence and pushed himself to participate in some clubs and even try out for the tennis team. He loved tennis and appreciated the athleticism the sport demanded. He could visualize himself as a varsity team player.

The friends he made the summer before high school were part of his posse beyond graduation. Mark Tilton and Joe Hefner were amazed at Ben's talents when they visited the family store to see what he had created with his father's guidance. They were constantly impressed with Ben's humility and skills.

Ben graduated from Indiana University with a degree in business…and relaxation. To say he enjoyed his college life would be an understatement—maybe it wasn't to the degree of Buddy

Stewart, but his five-year experience was memorable. For being such a mild-mannered guy, Ben surprised Mark and Joe when he shared his bong experience and love for a pepperoni-and-pineapple pizza, a double tequila chaser, and another hit on the bong.

Fifteen years after Ben's graduation from the university, his parents were tragically killed in an auto accident. Ben was understandably shaken but pledged to carry on the family dream of making a wonderful life in the greatest country in the world, just as his parents had told him to do on many occasions.

Ben and Marie were married in 1967, and they forged ahead toward the American dream his parents had wanted for him. The Schein Jewelry and Watch Repair Shop was fortunate to have solid footing and a profitable base in the 1970s.

It was Ben's wife, Marie, who would greet the customers as they entered their shop. Ben was now in the process of training a young man to assist on the sales side and learn some jewelry repair skills.

Ben's casual appearance and attire were legendary. Ben was about five feet, ten inches tall, maybe more than a little overweight. He had a bit of a combover. Large dark-rimmed glasses with a piece of white athletic tape on the nose piece and a Breathe Right strip were his facial trademark. Combined with a blue oversized zip-up cardigan sweater; gray polyester Sansabelt slacks; white, textured no-iron shirt; large striped tie with a full Windsor knot; and Velcro tennis shoes…that was Ben Schein.

For twelve years, the store was successful. Ben and Marie's hard work provided a comfortable lifestyle. But Marie died from a rare cancer in 2001. Ben was devastated and decided to retire.

He moved into Blue Ridge Vista, where T. Randall and Buddy were already living.

Salvatore Giuseppe Romano, or Sal, came to the United States with his parents in 1948 after his birth in Udine, Italy, the northernmost province in Italy. The Friuli-Venezia Guilia region borders the mountainous region of Austria. Sal's father, Vittorio, worked in a sawmill as operations manager, and his wife, Sophia, was a dedicated and loving inspiration to both Romano men.

The Romanos would have another child after arriving in America, but a rare and fatal illness would take the life of their daughter, Sal's sister, at the age of four. The loss of Maria crushed the Romano family as they continued to make their way in their new world.

Being in a new country and city and learning a new language shaped the way the Romano family would cope in their daily lives. Vittorio and Sophia focused all their love and nurturing on Sal. The Romanos lived a simple life. Vittorio was able to find a good job with a lumber company, and his prior work experience and training in northern Italy proved valuable to him and his employer. Vittorio's knowledge of operating and processing equipment was instrumental and enabled his new employer to expand their business in the wholesale distribution of equipment and parts that were made in Italy and Europe.

Although trying to learn English in a new workplace presented a challenge, Vittorio's new employer was patient and rewarded his contributions with a promotion and more responsibilities. The import business of machinery and equipment proved to be profitable for the Harold and Sons Lumber Company.

The Romanos lived in a modest yet impeccably neat home. Sal's chores and house duties were made clear by his father: taking out the trash, tidying the yard, cleaning his bedroom, helping his mother, completing his studies—this is what Sal's father expected, and Sal knew it. There was no gray area to complicate expectations. Vittorio was a man of few words and deliberate conversation, a trait that Sal would acquire and elevate to a new level as he grew and matured.

Vittorio's hobbies of fine carpentry and winemaking would become part of Sal's persona.

The Romanos' basement included a laundry area, a carpentry and woodworking space, and a corner for winemaking, a skill Vittorio had learned from his parents in Italy. Each fall, Sal would accompany his father to the produce yard to choose the grapes for their wine. Vittorio used two red grape varietals and one white that would increase the alcohol content of the finished product. The Romanos used a wooden hand press, which had a large threaded screw attached to a wooden plate and a handle on top to squeeze the juice out of the grapes. It took a long time to crush ninety crates of grapes to fill the wooden barrel. Their basement never smelled as good as it did in the fall during the fermentation process.

Sal loved the time he spent with his father, who, while stern, always encouraged Sal to enjoy life and be respectful and willing to help those in need but not be taken advantage of.

The Romanos would do their best to speak English in their home, but inevitably as the subject matter turned complex, Italian was spoken. The most enjoyable time together was over the simplest family tasks: making pasta, tasting the wine before bottling, and walking to church for Sunday mass.

Vittorio would pass away at the age of seventy-five, and within a year, Sophia died of cancer. Sal's memories were his comfort and source of strength; he knew how his parents had worked to make a better life for him.

Sal married Regina Cappelletti, and they had two children, Antonio and Flavia. Regina would die from COVID-19. By this time, Sal and his family had settled in south-central Pennsylvania, about an hour and a half from Uniontown. Sal's children now lived on opposite coasts in the United States. Sal decided he did not need the larger home he had built and made the move to an independent senior living community about forty-five minutes from Washington, DC, in the rolling hills of Virginia.

Buddy had been living at Blue Ridge Vista longer than the other Knights. Just before the national scare of COVID, Buddy had accepted the real estate sales position, and along with his new job, he was able to negotiate a model unit. The downside was that he had to keep it clean...all the time.

Ben arrived at Blue Ridge Vista shortly after Buddy. The COVID lockdown was a great opportunity for Ben to focus on documenting his family's history, journey to America, and life in Indiana. His work was a labor of love and pride.

Sal arrived at Blue Ridge Vista within a month of Ben. As it did for Ben, COVID meant a change in his normalcy. Sal spent his spare time building his grape arbors, flower boxes, and planters for his tomatoes and vegetables. He enjoyed gardening almost as much as carpentry.

Like Ben, Sal had treasured his family's journey to America. He proudly displayed his photo collection on the shelves and tables of his patio home. Each photo had a beautiful story. There were dates and names on the back of each photo that helped to memorialize the Romano family history. There was one shelf devoted to several pictures of his beautiful wife, a gorgeous woman whose beauty was matched only by her kindness and generosity.

For Buddy, Ben, and Sal, COVID had forced them into seclusion while the pandemic made its way across the nation. They knew one another, but not well. The Blue Ridge Vista health guidelines were enough to reinforce everything they had been watching on the national news. They resented the lockdowns but feared more for their lives. They were able to enjoy the beauty of Blue Ridge Vista but not the camaraderie of one another—not yet.

T. Randall was the last to make his way to Blue Ridge Vista. Like Buddy, Ben, and Sal, T. Randall was unpacking memories, some more painful than others. He still bore tremendous resentment about his departure from his law firm, but he needed to move on with his life. He needed a new focus, and he was about to have it and more. His former law firm would shortly understand that paybacks are a bitch.

Chapter Two:

DEMETRIUS LORENZO WILSON

"Mr. Refken, I assure you that if this proposed arrangement that you have outlined does not work to the satisfaction of this court, you will be looking for new employment, understood? Your wardrobe will be the least of your concerns."

Judge Carmichael's court was in the middle of Washington, DC, not exactly a garden spot. The courtroom was dated by the dark walnut paneling, circa 1940. Large oil paintings of judges from the thirties, forties, and fifties filled the massive panels to the side of his bench. The courtroom was full, the judge recognizing many of the faces he had met on prior occasions. On this day, the judge had twenty-five cases on the docket; Demitrius was first.

"Your honor," Demetrius's attorney, Julius Refken, said. "Enough about my clothes, please. I will do whatever I can to help my client, out of tremendous respect for his grandmother. Blue Ridge Vista is not far from where I live, and I would be happy to be a part of the team to help Demetrius in this process."

"Mr. Refken, this court appreciates your willingness and desire to help in this matter. If you are certain and confident about your recommendation, this court will agree.

"Demetrius Lorenzo Wilson, this court sentences you to three years of electronically monitored probation served at the Blue Ridge Vista Living Community. You are subject to random substance tests, and you will be visited by a court-appointed representative to evaluate your progress. Should you for any reason fail to comply with this court's directives or the rules of the facility where you will be staying, you will serve a sentence of five years in county jail.

"Do you understand this ruling and these terms?"

"Yeah," Demetrius, known as De-Lo, said.

"What did you say? I could not hear your response," replied the judge.

"Yes, Your Honor," De-Lo said.

"You will be escorted to Blue Ridge Vista by this court today. You are permitted to have five minutes with your grandmother before you are transported."

And with the judge's ruling, De-Lo's life was about to change in a way he could not comprehend.

Charles (Chuck) Layton was that guy in grade school who always wanted to endear himself to the teacher, regardless of what he did. This also made him the target of his other classmates, which he totally deserved. Whether he was telling the teacher about misbehaving students or trying to push in front the of girls in line to get to lunch, he made enemies with ease. At recess, girls and boys found ways to make Charles regret his behavior. Charles was not a happy camper. Years later, Chuck found a career to make his grade school memories vanish. He became a probation officer, able to exert his childlike behavior on those who had just had a bad judicial experience. Chuck was now the king in his own little fiefdom, or at least he thought.

Chuck listened intently to Judge Carmichael's ruling, convinced he could make De-Lo have a miserable stay at Blue Ridge

Vista. Chuck would discover that he had made another incorrect character assessment.

Chuck's security badge rested comfortably on his forty pounds of extra stomach, which was pushed to the limit in a size-too-small county-issued khaki shirt. His dark-blue snagged polyester pants did not fit any better, and along with black soft-sole shoes with worn-off heels, they made a striking mental image. He looked like a large stuffed sausage. His slovenly appearance was not enhanced by his challenged hygiene and his attitude. His hair was long, especially his foraging nasal hair. His skin had a glow and not from cleanliness. His leg weighed more than De-Lo. But for now, De-Lo was going to be under Chuck's supervision, at least temporarily.

There was no doubt that De-Lo had made some stupid decisions and hung around with bad characters. The truth was, De-Lo was smart but lacked self-confidence; he went along to get along.

Last Friday night, what little luck he had was gone. De-Lo was supposed to be the lookout on the corner. Javon, a friend since grade school, was going to break into a bakery's back door, smash the cash drawer, grab the green, and be gone. With the increase in neighborhood crime, business owners were tired of getting robbed. On this night, Marco Santini, the bakery owner, decided to sleep in his back room with a shotgun just in case an intruder decided to break into his shop. Javon used a crowbar to break in, but unknown to De-Lo, he also had a 9mm Glock hidden in his waistband.

The noise of the cracking door jamb and Marco catching a glimpse of a handgun was all he needed to fire a shot in the direction of the intruder, hitting Javon on the shoulder. De-Lo scrambled to get a badly bleeding Javon out of the shop as fast as he could. He dragged Javon to the closest emergency room, over a block away, saving his life in the process.

When the emergency room staff questioned De-Lo on how this "accident" had occurred, his story made no sense, and certainly not to the police who were waiting in the outside hallway.

Another police unit was at the bakery getting a report and description of the burglars.

Marco's detailed description of the intruders left no doubt. Both were going to jail.

The three-strikes law meant both men were going to have a new home for a minimum of ten years. De-Lo would fare better, as his grandmother Rose's appeal to the judge provided the sway to have him sent to Blue Ridge Vista under court supervision.

Rose, now seventy-eight, was a remarkable woman. She had worked two jobs most of her life as a single mother of three children. Shontee, De-Lo's mom, had two children: Levi and De-Lo. Shontee battled drugs since she was eighteen, and De-Lo came to know Rose as his mother. Subsidized housing in the projects presented its own challenges to De-Lo's search for some type of normalcy in his life. Rose did her best, and De-Lo knew it.

Judge Carmichael felt Rose's pain in his courtroom when he saw her slap De-Lo in the face for being disrespectful.

"I know we didn't have much, but I raised you better than this. I apologize, Judge. He knows I don't tolerate that attitude in my house, and I'm sure as hell not going to put up with it here," she said.

De-Lo was introduced to his parole officer, Chuck Layton, a real gem of a bureaucratic failure. Chuck casually walked up behind De-Lo as Judge Carmichael was reviewing the paperwork to be processed for the hearing. He quietly spoke into De-Lo's ear.

"Listen, boy, I am going to be so far up your ass that your tonsils are going to hurt. Got it? One fuckup, and I am personally going to drive you to the county jail, and I can't wait. I will give you one week, maybe two, at the most. Enjoy Blue Ridge Vista for the short time you'll be there."

Oddly enough, De-Lo believed him and began to wonder and question how he was going to make it. De-Lo was smart, and he had received good grades in math and reading when he went to school. He hid his intelligence to fit in and be a part of his gang, and now he realized how stupid that was.

What in the hell was he going to do at Blue Ridge Vista with a bunch of old crackers who smelled and wet the bed? He had no options and sure didn't want to go to the county jail. He was going to try to make it work, somehow.

Judge Carmichael's judicial discernment told him that De-Lo was not a bad guy even though he made bad decisions. The judge had been doing this for twenty years, and his instincts seldom let him down. The fact that Javon asked his court-appointed attorney to tell Judge Carmichael the truth about what happened that night and that De-Lo had no idea about the gun helped the judge decide to send De-Lo to Blue Ridge Vista.

The door of the police van opened, and Chuck Layton removed De-Lo's handcuffs, making sure the ankle monitor was secure and working. He turned to De-Lo.

"Remember what I said. One to two weeks at the most. I'm going to visit you in one week to do the personal evaluation that Judge Carmichael ordered. Hope you fuck up. I will get a daily ten-panel screen result through the resident doctor's office here at Blue Ridge Vista. You'll never make it."

And with that, Chuck was gone.

De-Lo was escorted to the back entrance by the delivery dock for the maintenance shop. There, he met the assistant director of facilities for Blue Ridge Vista, Ruiz Gonzales. The Department of Corrections required an assessment of all new placements to determine their work skills, if any, and their ability to get along with the other employees. Ruiz had seen many De-Los in his day and wasn't willing to make any bets on how he thought his time at Blue Ridge Vista would work out.

De-Lo had his own room, and although small, it was a significant improvement over his bedroom in subsidized housing and his own locker in the maintenance shop. He also received a uniform, towels, washcloths, and toiletries. He immediately took a shower.

Ruiz had a daily, weekly, and monthly work schedule already charted. De-Lo's first week was with the janitorial team. Following breakfast, he went to the assisted living section of Blue Ridge Vista to work in the common area. He would be vacuuming and mopping floors on his first day of freedom. Whose idea was this? He studied the faces and movements of the geriatric crowd, wondering whether this would be the way he would spend the rest of his time at Blue Ridge Vista.

De-Lo saw Rose's face in the other women in the common area, and suddenly he was overcome by a rush of anxiety. He paused to take a few deep breaths and regained his focus. What stupid decisions he'd made, and he had dumped his bad decisions on his grandmother. She certainly didn't deserve to be worried and fearful for De-Lo at her age. That was on him.

After dinner, De-Lo walked the grounds outside the maintenance area. He saw a guy and casually waved to him. He would later discover that the guy was Sal Romano.

For the next week, De-Lo's work schedule was the same. Without his knowledge, he was being monitored on the facility surveillance cameras. It was better for De-Lo that he didn't know. It was also an opportunity for Ruiz to assess and take notes for his file to be reviewed by De-Lo's probation officer.

Week three was the same for De-Lo. It was by design to see if De-Lo had the initiative to ask for a different work assignment, which he did. De-Lo asked to speak with Ruiz about an idea he had been considering. When De-Lo had met Sal briefly on his walk, he noticed some things outside while he was working in the common area. Blue Ridge Vista's architectural style was classic traditional: red brick, white limestone corners and windowsills and headers, and excellent carpentry with twenty-foot-tall columns on the front of the veranda. For such a beautiful place, the carpeting, the painting, and the shrubs and grounds needed work to make the property look better.

De-Lo asked to work with the outside maintenance crew. Ruiz said yes and placed him with the foreman for the grounds. He would cut grass, prune shrubs, pick up sticks, spread mulch, and do any other task that the foreman demanded. De-Lo didn't mind at all and enjoyed working outside.

He met Sal and Ben briefly as he was lifting a bag of mulch from the back of the maintenance truck. This time, they each introduced themselves. De-Lo enjoyed the interaction and thought these old guys were OK.

De-Lo smiled and said, "See you guys around."

Sal and Ben walked back to their patio homes. By this time, Sal and Ben had already shared their own personal family stories with each other. Sal loved Ben's casual demeanor and his unique laughter, which was a loud and jovial outburst. Sal had arrived at Blue Ridge Vista about two months before Ben, and they were glad to have each other to walk and talk with on the grounds.

Buddy had been working at Blue Ridge Vista for about nine months, and Sal and Ben learned that he had sold so many of the units that Blue Ridge Vista was planning an expansion on the north side of the property. Buddy was asked to slow down until the design architect could complete his rendering of the new homes. Buddy reluctantly agreed but was disappointed, as he was on a roll.

Willow Court was on a beautiful cul-de-sac about two hundred yards from the entrance of Blue Ridge Vista. The homes were red brick with white architectural accents that complemented the main Blue Ridge Vista Pavilion. Faux-stone sidewalks lent a perfect touch along with the tree-lined median. Their yards were meticulously manicured. It was picture perfect. Best of all, they were only fifty yards from each other.

The next morning, a moving van arrived early. The new resident on Willow Court was a quiet man named T. Randall Kaufman II. He was tall, thin, and distinguished, not a hair out of place. He wore Italian Ferragamo loafers that Sal had seen in a catalogue some time ago and knew he couldn't afford; besides, his feet were too fat. Ben, Sal, and Buddy thought his name was too long, so they gave him the nickname T, unbeknownst to him. Sal decided to take a bottle of homemade wine over to T the next evening, and they would all welcome him to the neighborhood.

The patio homes had spacious backyards for a facility of this type. Sal had built a beautiful arbor as a home for his transplanted grapes, just enough to make a small supply of wine to enjoy in his new home and share with friends. Over fifty years, Sal had learned the art of winemaking from his parents, from the types of grapes to use to the ratios to achieve the best results. The Virginia climate was ideal. The evenings and mornings provided the perfect balance, cool and dry. The sunlight stressed the grapes to reinforce the flavor, and the soil needed to be dry as well. Sal had studied a lot over the years. He grew the Alicante grape as the foundation, as well as a Cabernet Sauvignon varietal. These rich bold, fruity, and aromatic flavors made for perfect blending grapes. Sal would add white grapes, which contained a higher sugar level and increased the alcohol content of the finished wine. Within the last fifteen years, Sal even experimented with potassium metabisulphite and yeast to increase the shelf life of his wine. Sal had to admit to himself that the new method in the winemaking process had proven a wise decision. His new wines were excellent.

Sal could remember the time he first tasted his grandmother's wine. He was only thirteen.

One little sip, and beads of sweat formed on his forehead; he never forgot the sensation.

Sal had three six-gallon buckets that he used in the fermentation process. An old wine press made the juicing process easier. He couldn't wait until Labor Day to begin harvesting his grapes. He now had friends to share it with, and that was even better.

Ben was more the historian type. His family's trek through small towns in Hungary, Austria, and Italy had been documented by his parents' letters and photos. COVID had given him the time to arrange his story chronologically with his own comments from other family members. Ben's work was a labor of love and respect. He was surprised at how much he had re-membered from all the family get-togethers. He was proud of his work and displayed a leather-bound volume of the Schein family history on the table in the living room. He had chosen a black-and-white family photo when he was about five years old to display next to the book.

According to Ben's parents, the photo was from a stop they had made in Austria on their journey to America.

Buddy was an avid sports fan; prized memorabilia was on display the moment you entered his home. Leroy Neiman prints of athletes and sporting events, NBA and NFL jerseys from the stars of the fifties, sixties, seventies, and eighties decorated the walls, and ticket stubs from playoff games in baseball and hockey were under glass on tables in clear view for any fan. Buddy's favorite sport was football; his favorite team was the Chicago Bears. The 1985 Super Bowl Champs banner had a special place over his fireplace along with an autographed team picture, his most prized possession. He knew every stat from that team for the entire year and was glad to share them with you, whether you wanted to hear or not. A normal conversation would start something like this as he saw you staring at the banner:

"Hey, let me tell you something about the eighty-five Bears that you don't know." The only thing you could do was listen, because he wouldn't stop talking.

T's patio home was more sterile in style. Law books were on display on the shelves in his entryway along with individual pic-tures of his children, but none of his wife. There were beautiful paintings in oils and watercolors that the other Knights would discover were very expensive. You would never know because T never talked about it. Classical music was his preference, al-though on occasion you could hear some light jazz—nothing too wild. There were pictures of T with politicians that the Knights easily recognized, which were not in prominent view.

T's story was sad in so many ways. His family and his law practice—the firm his father had founded—were all gone. Little did he realize how much he would enjoy the friendship of Ben, Sal, and Buddy. They had nothing in common but themselves.

Sal noticed that De-Lo was now working with the grounds crew, so when he saw him the following week, they exchanged greetings and spent a little more time getting to know each other. Sal shared some things about his family and where he came from, but De-Lo was reluctant and embarrassed to share his background. Even though he sensed that Sal was easy to talk to,

De-Lo feared Sal would judge him and end their brief friendship. De-Lo could not have been more wrong.

"Hey, good morning, De-Lo. What's up?"

"Sup, Sal? What it be?"

"What?" asked Sal. "What it be?"

"C'mon, Holmes, you know, da! 'What are you doing?' in English."

"I was just checking to see how you're getting along."

"It's all good," said De-Lo. "Another beautiful day at BRV."

"Oh, BRV—Blue Ridge Vista. That's pretty cool, De-Lo."

"Just chillin' to some sounds, you know."

"What kinda sounds?" asked Sal.

"Rap, hip-hop be my melody. Know what I mean?"

"Not really, De-Lo. Wish I did, but my mind can't keep up with it. Sorry."

"Not to worry, Sal; it's all good. How 'bout you, Sal? How do you get your groove on?"

"My 'groove on'? Help me out, De-Lo; not sure I get it."

"Oh, you get it; you just don't know it."

"Not followin' you, De-Lo."

"What the heck you like, Sal? I mean music. What makes you chill?"

"I mean, I like rock, soul, the old guys, country—you know, just normal stuff."

"Normal? C'mon Sal, you know some of that shit will make you crazy. I mean, tell me your favorite soul crew. I had you for a Sinatra kinda guy. I heard him on a video one time. That old dude had some pipes, really. Know what I mean?"

"I do know what you mean, De-Lo. I really enjoyed Ol' Blue Eyes. He was more a part of my parents' generation. But I will tell you, when he sang, 'My Way,' I loved it, every single time."

"That's cool. I get it, but, like, after Frankie, what cooks your grits?"

"That'd be the Temptations. I saw them in concert in Pittsburgh. Gave me goosebumps. I could listen to them all day. Maybe some Smokey and a little Four Tops, I'd be a happy man. OK?"

"OK, OK, that's pretty cool, I mean, for an old dude."

Sal just grinned. "Tell me, De-Lo, what brings you to Blue Ridge Vista?" De-Lo paused for a moment, embarrassed by the truth.

"I got here in a van…from the Department of Corrections, and that's the truth."

"Sorry, none of my business," said Sal. "You seem like a good guy, and thanks for not laughing at my music."

De-Lo shook his head, thought for a moment, and enjoyed a quiet laugh himself. Sal was different from what he imagined a guy his age would be. Things could be a lot worse.

De-Lo had shared his circumstances with Sal, who listened intently, and that surprised De-Lo and made him feel less vulnerable. Sal just said he enjoyed talking with him and hoped the two would talk again soon. Sal casually walked back to his new home.

Chapter Three:

The First Meeting

Buddy had talked with Sal and Ben about inviting T for a more casual get-together. They agreed that it would be a way for all of them to learn a little bit more about one another and a reason to have a small glass of wine and some great Italian cheese, sausage, pepperoni, and more. Sal and Ben were all in.

Sal walked over to T's house and knocked on the door, trying to think of just the right greeting. As T opened the door, Sal froze and stared at T. "Man, you're tall. I mean tall."

Considering that Sal was a shade over five feet, nine inches, T was every bit six foot three or four inches, as best he could figure. Sal just looked up like he was staring at a large telephone pole.

"OK," said T. Randall. "Thank you, I guess."

"You look like a male model. Do you dress that nice all the time?"

"It depends."

"On what?" asked Sal. "Where I'm going."

"I wanted to invite you to my place tonight to meet Buddy and Ben around six o'clock, if that works for you. You don't really need to dress so fancy—don't get me wrong, you look good; you can dress any way you want. Hope you can make it."

"I would love to. Thank you for the invitation. Looking forward to meeting Buddy and Ben and getting to know you all better."

"Great," said Sal, "see you then." Sal had managed to stumble through another invitation, but this time it was a real shit show. He didn't have to comment on T's height, even though he was very tall, or his clothes, even though he was well dressed. He could only imagine what T was thinking, and he was sure it was not that flattering.

Sal had decided his usual clothes—tan khaki pants, plaid shirt, and brown work shoes—might need an upgrade. Sal dressed like this almost every day, sometimes with a light-blue button-down-collar shirt or a blue-and-white pinstripe shirt, but that was the extent of Sal's daily wardrobe.

Sal headed back to his house to get ready for the get-together, wanting to make sure everything was just right.

T. Randall had unpacked his boxes and turned the smaller bedroom of his patio home into an office, where he could maintain some semblance of order in his new living space and the next chapter of his life. The unpacking was like picking off a scab that you had been touching and scratching for weeks; you knew it was going to hurt, but you had to do it.

The family photos started the downhill slide for T. A lifetime of memories—birthdays, holidays, vacations, a second family home—sat in one of the boxes.

One of the photos he gazed at for a while was the last law firm picture, from a retreat about five years ago. The firm had added some newer and much younger partners, who, in a short time, made names for themselves. T couldn't remember all their names but did recollect some of their major wins and transactions.

T stopped the pain after less than ten minutes. He decided to go for a walk and get his mind going in a different direction. A long walk would clear his mind and give him the chance to appreciate his new home and surroundings at Blue Ridge Vista. The original owners had done an incredible job of ensuring and preserving the integrity of the property. Blue Ridge Vista was beautiful and well planned. It should be, because he remembered how the PE group out of Boston had jumped in at the last moment and offered 25 percent more to secure the deal with "no contingencies." Who could afford to do something like that? He also remembered that the real estate firm had paid for a phenomenal number of services to help secure the deal for the other buyer.

He walked for half an hour on the gently rolling grounds, taking in the real beauty of the property. He thought that this was going to work out OK. He would go to the main office in the morning to personally meet the leadership team of Blue Ridge Vista and listen to their presentation about all the amenities and services.

He had just enough time to shower before joining the others at Sal's.

Sal decided to prepare some salami, prosciutto, and cheese for the gathering. He had heard of an Italian deli in the nearby town and decided to try it. The owner was from a region in Italy near the home of Sal's parents. They spoke in Italian, and Sal enjoyed sampling the excellent meats and cheeses. Sal had hit the jackpot; the deli was less than ten minutes from his new home. Life at Blue Ridge Vista was going to be OK.

Ben was first to arrive, and he joined Sal in the kitchen while he was preparing the antipasto. He couldn't resist trying some samples while Sal was reaching into the refrigerator. Without missing a beat, Sal spoke.

"How do you like the antipasto?" he asked as Ben was sampling the prosciutto and asiago cheese.

Ben just laughed in his loud voice. "This is great," he replied. "I'm glad you like it," said Sal, closing the fridge door.

"Me too," said Ben.

Buddy didn't even knock. He opened the door and walked in. "Hello! Where in the hell are you guys?"

"In the kitchen," Sal and Ben replied in unison. "Where's T?"

"We got to give him time. I'm sure he'll be here soon," Ben said. They heard a knock at the door.

"C'mon in; the door's unlocked," Buddy said.

T. Randall stepped into the foyer and looked around. "I hope I got the right place. Is this Sal's house?" he said.

"Sure is," said Buddy. "Sal and Ben are in the kitchen. C'mon in and make yourself at home."

"Hey, you guys," Buddy yelled into the kitchen. "T is here. What the heck are you doing in there?"

"Be patient; almost done," said Sal. "Why don't you come into the kitchen? There's enough room for us to visit here."

Buddy was not bashful when it came to joining a gathering. He got to the kitchen first. "Where's T?" Sal asked.

"He's probably casing out your living room to see if you have anything worth stealing," replied Buddy, laughing and hoping T was not too sensitive. And with that, T walked into the kitchen.

Sal greeted him first. "Nice to meet you, T. I'm Sal Romano, and this is Ben Schein. The screamer you heard was Buddy Stewart."

"Please excuse me," T. Randall said. "Who is T?"

"That'd be you," said Buddy. "We thought your name was too long and thought it would be easier to call you T. What do you think?"

"I'm not sure; nobody ever decided to change my name or give me a new one. I'll have to think about it."

"We're not really changing your name, just shortening it. Give it time; we think you'll like it." And with that Ben leaned forward to greet T with his usual loud laugh and caught T off guard.

"Nice to meet you, T," Ben said.

"Did you find anything in Sal's living room worth stealing?" asked Buddy.

A look of astonishment overcame T's red face, his eyebrows arched, and his eyes grew huge.

"I know I checked it out before you got here, and I have my eye on the neat glass sphere on Sal's bookshelf," said Buddy.

Sal shook his head, and Ben laughed loudly. Buddy smiled.

"Welcome to the neighborhood," Sal said as he poured four small jelly jars full of homemade wine, raised his glass to all of them, and said, "*Salud, mangia*—that's 'to your health' and 'eat' in Italian."

They sat down at the round table in Sal's kitchen, with the large cutting board in the middle with salami, cheese, marinated olives, roasted red peppers, and fresh bread ready to be devoured.

Chapter Four:

Probation Continues

Chuck Layton was five minutes away from Blue Ridge Vista. It was the middle of De-Lo's third week of working with the facilities team. As surprised as Chuck was, he remained confident that De-Lo would screw up and be headed to county jail in no time.

When he arrived, Chuck looked for De-Lo without checking in with Ruiz. That was a mistake. Ruiz saw Chuck walk up behind De-Lo and start to interrogate him in front of other employees and residents of Blue Ridge Vista. Ruiz lit into Chuck and embarrassed him in the same way Chuck had tried to intimidate De-Lo.

"What the hell do you think you are doing?" asked Ruiz. "I'm doing my job; it's not your business," said Chuck. Wrong answer and a big mistake, Ruiz thought.

"Bullshit," said Ruiz. "De-Lo is under my supervision here at Blue Ridge Vista. If you want to talk with him, you ask me."

"Judge Carmichael knows I'm here, so if you have a problem, tell it to the judge," Chuck said mockingly.

"I'll call Judge Carmichael's office now and tell him how you tried to intimidate De-Lo in front of all these folks, and let's see what he says. Sound good to you?"

"You don't need to do that. I just wanted to see how things are going for him at Blue Ridge Vista as part of my work for the court," Chuck said.

"I'll tell you what: the next time you want to see how things are going, you call me, make an appointment, and I'll see if I can work you in, got it? Otherwise, you can find another person to harass," said Ruiz.

"My report to the judge is not going to look good for you or De-Lo," said Chuck.

Ruiz walked over to Chuck and quietly talked into his ear. "Tell you what, you piece of shit. We have you on video, you stupid fool, so you make sure your report coincides with the video that I can share with Judge Carmichael, who called me before you got here. Do you understand, Chuck?"

De-Lo was stunned. Ruiz was the second person who had reached out to try to help him. He wasn't used to this treatment. At the same time, he realized that Chuck was embarrassed and would be looking for the smallest infraction to make his life more miserable. He wanted to do what he was supposed to do and avoid getting in any trouble.

As De-Lo turned to thank Ruiz for his intervention, he noticed Chuck making a beeline for his car.

Ruiz had a brief talk with De-Lo to put his mind at ease and to let him know that he did have some people at Blue Ridge Vista he could talk to.

"Just keep doing what you are doing, take pride in what you do, and be willing to help someone when they need it. You're doin' a good job, De-Lo. Keep it up," Ruiz said.

Wow, De-Lo thought. It was almost time for lunch. De-Lo would head back to the shop area after stopping by the kitchen to get his meal. He had a lot to think about.

Next week, he would be working in food service, in the kitchen washing pots and pans, and he didn't mind.

The first gathering of T, Buddy, Ben, and Sal was uneventful. They all shared stories about their lives, their families, and how they arrived at Blue Ridge Vista. Sal listened intently, as he had a vision that they would be the protectors of their new home, Blue Ridge Vista. Sal had been making notes about the general conditions of the property, both inside and out, that he hadn't shared with them yet.

Buddy and T discovered that they had something in common: Blue Ridge Vista. While Buddy had been stiffed on the transaction, T's practice raked in millions of dollars in professional fees from the original sale. The entire transaction still haunted Buddy in so many ways. "No contingencies." Who in their right mind could afford to do that deal? He knew the amount of work his team did and how long it took to coordinate all the services. His team and their attorney only had two days to review each set of services and the opinions of other attorneys, and they weren't anywhere near done when the other offer was presented and accepted.

"You know, T, when the Blue Ridge Vista transaction was going down, I couldn't believe that someone could offer that much money and...*no contingencies*. Who does that crap? I mean, how much freaking money do those guys have?"

"As it turned out, Buddy, they got burned, the kind of burn that cost several guys their fancy jobs. We learned that a former EverStar exec had enough information on the deal to make him dangerous. What he didn't realize was how complex the whole deal was and what EverStar had constructed as a masterplan.

A major residential development, a gated community with a championship golf course, and most important, a major federal spend on a highway bypass to make the DC drive to Blue Ridge Vista only twenty minutes. EverStar had done a lot of work internally to keep that a secret."

"Holy crap, T. How big are we talking?" asked Buddy.

"Based on what we were told, north of eight hundred million dollars for Blue Ridge Vista and billions for the road construction. I mean, their political connections were told to be on standby. EverStar owns guys on both sides of the aisle, from what we knew. This was going to be a blockbuster transaction. Once COVID surfaced, EverStar got the deal out of receivership for pennies on the dollar. Our firm got a big retainer, and I was forced out of the law practice my father started. It really sucked."

"I'm sorry for what happened to you, T, really. Just so you know, I got stiffed twice on the same transaction. The guy who I agreed to cobroker with on the deal didn't pay me, and my wife embezzled three million dollars from my practice. She split to the Bahamas with a guy who I helped get started in real estate sales. Talk about the shits."

"Unbelievable. My God," said T. "I wish I could do something for you."

"I'm doing my best to stay focused on some of the better times," said Buddy. "I gotta tell you, T, your firm had a great reputation in the DC market. I heard your name many times. Other agents would talk about your attention to the smallest detail and your impeccable appearance: never a hair out of place and always the finest suits. They were right. You still got it."

"Thank you, Buddy. That's very kind of you to say."

Sal had had the opportunity to see many of Ben's family photos when he was invited to have some coffee at his home. He never had a chance to talk with him about how his family had escaped the Germans in Romania and how they made it through Europe.

"Ben, if you don't mind telling me, how was your family able to flee Europe? It must have been scary."

"You know, Sal, the stories my parents and grandparents told me were unbelievable. They were frightened for their lives every day. The Germans hated the Jews; many still do, I'm sad to say. I was told that my grandparents would pay what little money they had for the name of a person in some town who they could ask for help. They believed in a network of very distantly related cousins and cousins of cousins to make their escape. It worked, thank God."

"Your family must have been very brave. Everything I have read about Hitler disgusts me. His hatred for Jews created a monster who cost millions of lives," Sal said apologetically.

"Sal, you don't know how many times I quietly say a prayer of thanks to my parents and grandparents for their courage to leave Romania and make America my new home. I am blessed by God, and I know it. I'm also glad that I have met you, Buddy, and T."

"I feel the exact same way, Ben. You know, it's funny how the four of us have come together at Blue Ridge Vista. I mean, who could have figured? I'm just glad we did."

"Me too," said Ben. "Another blessing. You know, Sal, I never really cared for Mondays, but now I think Mondays are going to be great."

They had agreed to meet weekly on Mondays at 6:00 p.m. to recap their weekend and plan what they wanted to do over the next week. They also agreed to take a long walk and get the "lay of the land," as Buddy described it. "We need to check this place out for ourselves."

"Next week, we are going on a walk on Tuesday at ten a.m. We'll take some water with us and get some pictures. It'll be fun." It was decided.

Chapter Five:

THE PEBBLE IN DE-LO'S SHOE

I t was in the food service department where De-Lo encountered Sammy, a real smooth-talkin' scammer who he could tell was trouble. De-Lo kept his head down and did his work; there were a lot of pots and pans to clean after each meal.

"Hey, man, I guess you're new here. I'm Sammy, and I know you're De-Lo. Nice to meet you, brotha!" Sammy said. "You need anything, let me know, 'cause in this place, I'm da man...got it?"

"Yes, I got it," said De-Lo, keeping his head down while staring at the bubbles and all the pots and pans in the large double sink. He didn't need or want to deal with Sammy or any of the problems that were or would be Sammy. He just wanted to be left alone to do his work and try to figure a way out of Blue Ridge Vista.

De-Lo decided to ask Ruiz for five minutes to talk with him. Ruiz was not in charge of food service, but he was familiar with Sammy, as were other supervisors at Blue Ridge Vista.

De-Lo took a deep breath. He had only been at Blue Ridge for three weeks, but he felt he was making progress. He confided in Ruiz that Sammy was making him a bit uneasy, and he knew he could not afford a run-in with the guy.

"Any advice you could share, I sure would appreciate it," De-Lo said to Ruiz.

"My best advice is to be cordial but not friendly. Don't get dragged into his stuff. You are a smart kid, De-Lo, and as I said, you are doing a good job," Ruiz said. "I know that incident with Chuck was a bit embarrassing for you, but trust me, he got his ass handed to him by Judge Carmichael. I heard it was a thing of beauty.

"I know other supervisors and managers would love to see Sammy's ass out of here, but the problem is it would cost Blue Ridge way more money and attorney fees to get rid of him, and he probably knows it. We all have incident reports and other employee complaints about him that would keep human resources busy for weeks. They just don't want to deal with it, and they leave it to all the other supervisors to try to manage. I know he must be on thin ice but do yourself a favor and try to get along. I'll do my best to look out for you, OK?" Ruiz said.

"I appreciate you listening. Thank you," said De-Lo.

For now, De-Lo had a strategy. Avoidance was his pathway.

Chapter Six:

Meeting the & Team

During their Monday-evening visit, T had mentioned to Sal that he planned to schedule a meeting with the executive director and the management team to review his Blue Ridge Vista contract. He thought it would be better and more relaxing to review all the amenities of the facility. Sal had listened intently as T described what he was going to discuss. Without saying anything to T, Sal was going to review all of his own Blue Ridge Vista information as well and schedule a meeting with the executive team. If T had decided it was a good idea, Sal was convinced of the same. First, Sal would read through all his information again and make notes before the meeting.

Sal was relaxing in his living room reading *Italy, an Author's Journey*, an interesting read, especially the author's detailed stories of the towns and villages from the Friuli region down to the Adriatic coast. Sal had promised himself that he would return to the town and region where his family's life had begun. He was mesmerized momentarily and smiled.

He paused as he thought of his beautiful wife, Sophia, and the life they had made together. Sal had decided that he was going to try to make a difference while at Blue Ridge Vista, and he thought about the young man he briefly met, De-Lo, who was a likable guy with a nice demeanor. Sal would see what he could do for De-Lo if that was possible.

During their weekly walks around Blue Ridge Vista, the guys noticed little details around the buildings and the grounds, inside and outside, that needed repair. Sal made a mental note to add these to his list for his meeting with the executive director, which was in two days.

In the meantime, Sal had some grapevines to prune, and then he was going to meet with Ben. He had an idea and first wanted to run it by him because he knew Ben would listen and tell him the truth.

De-Lo had completed his fourth week at Blue Ridge Vista and was now going to be reassigned to the facility team, working on the main floor, the common area, and the executive corridor. He had passed the ten-panel drug screen with absolutely no trace of anything. He felt good about his physical condition. De-Lo had never gotten into drugs in a hard way, although he did enjoy weed, but to be honest, he didn't miss the hassle that came with it. He was even going to the employee fitness center, a privilege he had earned after three weeks. He felt good.

Ruiz gave him a heads-up on the executive corridor, where Blue Ridge Vista management services was located. He told De-Lo to stay focused, be polite, respond if spoken to, knock on a door, say "Facility crew," and smile. Sounds easy enough— nothing too difficult to remember,

De-Lo thought.

Ruiz was right. The first three days went well. On the fourth day, De-Lo caught the tail end of a conversation between some men and a woman who went off on what seemed like two of her bosses. Sounded a bit messy, talking about operating expense allocations and budget deficits, things he didn't understand, but he told Ruiz…and later, Sal and Ben.

De-Lo liked the action in that part of Blue Ridge Vista. Well-dressed adults engaged in spirited conversation and some humor. He just kept working…and listening. The last conversation he heard part of was that an annual report was due and needed to look better. As the next week went on, the volume of the discussion increased.

The cubicle he was cleaning was located next to a large conference room about ten feet away. The door was partially open. He heard the same woman, whose voice he recognized from the day before, say, "You assholes aren't going to make me the fall guy for this shit. I've been telling you about it for six months."

The other guy said, "You were supposed to transfer funds from the general funds to the operating budget because we had approval before that PE group started demanding the financials on a monthly basis. Now this is going to look like shit," he said.

And then De-Lo heard the guy in the big office say, "Look, it's going to be OK; trust me."

"And how in the hell do you know that?" the lady asked. "I just know it," he said.

The yelling continued for a while. De-Lo kept cleaning and listening. In a short time, he had learned a lot about Blue Ridge Vista. He wasn't sure what it meant, but it sounded interesting to a kid who was just trying to go along to get along, just like he did back in the hood. Only this time it wasn't as dangerous, or so he thought.

T had just finished his meeting with the executive team at Blue Ridge Vista, including Executive Director James Dillon, Assistant Director Abbey Connors, and CFO Michael Kennedy. They were aware of T. Randall Kaufman II's sway and influence in the DC area. He would be a much better ally than an enemy. He asked direct questions about the facility's financial footing and the owner's commitment to the longevity of the senior community. T was candid: this was his last move, not counting a funeral home and cemetery.

T noticed Abbey's body language when he asked James about Blue Ridge's financial stability. He noticed a twist in her neck but let it pass. He wanted to talk with Buddy, Sal, and Ben about the conversation to listen to their take and see whether they had learned anything more. Sal was going to meet with the same team again in two days, and he was curious to see whether James, Michael, and Abbey would have something different to share. T explained that he had asked his questions in a casual way, assuming there would be no surprises.

Sal had shared with Ben, Buddy, and T that he was going to ask about the facility's general appearance and condition, inside and out. Sal had not been at Blue Ridge Vista for a long time, but he had noticed a decline in the overall condition. He wanted to know whether his observations were warranted. Or was he just imagining? Sal was a smooth operator and was looking forward to the meeting.

On his way to meet with the executive team, Sal saw De-Lo in the common area with the janitorial crew. They exchanged greetings. Sal could sense that De-Lo wanted to stop and talk a bit, maybe catch up on some of the things that they had talked about in the past. Sal suggested that De-Lo talk to Ruiz and get his OK before De-Lo stopped the work he was doing. Sal did not want to be responsible for interrupting De-Lo's work. De-Lo agreed, said thank you, and continued heading toward the executive corridor.

Chapter Seven:

SAL THE PSYCHIATRIST

Sal let the receptionist know that he had an appointment with James, Abbey, and Michael. The receptionist explained that only Abbey would be available to talk with him. That was fine because Sal thought that would make the conversation a bit more casual. Boy was he wrong.

Abbey was fifteen minutes late without apologizing, only complaining about all the duties and responsibilities she had at Blue Ridge Vista.

"Mr. Romano, James, and Michael couldn't make the meeting, and they just called me ten minutes ago. This is not the way I would run things here at Blue Ridge Vista, you can be sure."

Sal sat quietly, listening to her rant.

"They probably got a golf game in and decided to make me do their work, one more time, like always," she continued.

Sal responded, "I can see you're having a rough day. Why don't I reschedule and come back when you're in better spirits? You look like you could use a break."

Sal's response tripped her trigger.

"What do you mean by that, Mr. Romano?"

"What do you mean, what do I mean?" Sal was sensing this meeting was about to head in a different direction; he remained calm. "I had planned to talk with James and Michael and you about some things I have noticed in the time I've been here at Blue Ridge Vista," he said.

"Well," said Abbey mockingly, "go ahead, old man, tell me about the things you noticed here at Blue Ridge Vista."

What an attitude, he thought. He took in a deep, slow breath, and paused, not wanting his temper to prove a problem one more time.

"You know, this is a bad idea. I'll come back," Sal said.

"Why? You don't think I can handle it because I'm a woman?" Abbey said. Sal pondered Abbey's response, biting his tongue.

"You know, if I had a penis, I'd be in charge of this place, and that's for sure," said Abbey. "Those two shitheads couldn't find their asses in a phone booth."

Sal thought it would be best to try to lighten the back-and-forth a bit. He cupped his hands and tilted his head to the side a bit as though to implore Abbey. "I'm not Dr. Phil or Dr. Laura, so I can't really help you with that, Abbey. You're on your own," Sal replied.

It might not have been the best response, but Abbey had gone into another zone completely.

"I wish I could help lower your stress. You seem like a nice person. You don't need the aggravation those guys are putting on you. Really, I can come back another time, OK?"

"No, no, it's not OK." Abbey pressed ahead, slightly relaxing but still mad as hell, not at Sal but at James and Michael. "I deserved that comment about Dr. Phil and Dr. Laura; that was pretty good, Sal. Please tell me what you have noticed about Blue Ridge Vista. I apologize for my outburst; it was inappropriate and unprofessional. I just get tired of covering for those jerks all the time."

"I certainly understand," said Sal. "It would be maddening to watch people not doing their jobs while they expect the day-to-day operations to run smoothly."

"Exactly," said Abbey. "Please, tell me what you are seeing around Blue Ridge Vista. I would like to know."

Sal related his observations about the interior and exterior painting, the clogged guttering, the frayed carpeting in the main dining area, and the landscaping. During Sal's six months at Blue Ridge Vista, the neglect was obvious.

Abbey listened and then shared with Sal that Blue Ridge Vista had just gone through a second reorganization. Abbey then told Sal more of the details.

"The original buyer, a private equity group out of Boston, had gone bankrupt following COVID-19 and some allegations of Medicare fraud. The new owner, EverStar, recently acquired Blue Ridge Vista for a fraction of the original cost and established two LLCs: one to operate the health-care operation and the other one to control the eight hundred and fifty acres of the remaining property. Our understanding is that a third party will control the health-care operation, and that is what has been most frustrating to me.

"James and Michael are making financial decisions without me being a part of the conversation. All I do is clean up their messes because they are clueless. I have documented everything since financial responsibilities were added to my assistant director's role nine months ago. James and Michael didn't want to pay the salary for another person, so they increased my workload. They are comingling operations and general funds with other accounts. It's a nightmare, and they don't care. They just say everything is OK, and it's not."

"How can I help you?" Sal asked.

"I appreciate you listening. Thank you," said Abbey. "I will investigate everything you shared with me and get back to you."

"Thank you very much," said Sal as he stood to make his way back to his home. He turned to Abbey. "You've gotta give yourself a chance to do something nice for you, know what I mean? What you described would make anyone pissed, if you'll excuse my language. Take care."

Sal could appreciate Abbey's frustration in dealing with James and Michael. Abbey was a type-A personality. From what Sal thought, she understood the financial management of Blue Ridge Vista better than both of them. She also knew that James and Michael were trying to hide information from her, and she was smart enough to know how and where to find it, which she did. Sal was slightly aware of the recent acquisition of Blue Ridge Vista by the EverStar Group, but what he heard didn't sound good to him. He would have to share his intel with the Knights for their take on the situation. He was also going to keep in close contact with Abbey. She knew what was going on and how it would affect the future of Blue Ridge Vista.

Chapter Eight:

THE ROUND TABLE

Sal thought he had pushed Abbey too much, but as he reflected on their meeting, he realized again that he was right—that Abbey was the person on the executive team who cared most about Blue Ridge Vista. Now the question was what the Knights were going to do to help her and help themselves.

Sal prepared more food, as he thought this meeting was probably going to take a bit longer than their previous ones.

Within five minutes, Ben, T, and Buddy were gathered in Sal's living room making some casual conversation. Sal loved the way they had lightened up, letting themselves into his house without thinking of ringing the doorbell.

They could smell the aroma of the cheese, sausage, and garlic in the kitchen and worked their way in, greeting Sal as his back was to them.

"Got any beer to start?" Buddy asked.

"Yeah, look on the top shelf in the refrigerator. Help yourself," Sal replied. "Man, Sal, this looks great, and I'm hungry," said Ben.

"You've come to the right place, Ben. *Mangiamo!*" Sal said.

Even T had lightened up. He was more at ease with himself and with the guys. Sal was glad because he sensed that T was dealing with some heavy stuff that challenged his ability to relax, but he was making progress.

Then there was Buddy—what a guy. Sal wished he had more of Buddy's personality. He was cool, a handsome guy who made you feel great when he talked with you. He had a real gift. Ben was the quiet type, although extremely interesting and smart. His attire and laughter were what Sal loved the most about Ben. He made you feel good.

Sal paused, pretending to look in the fridge just to hear them talk and laugh and enjoy themselves. He was so glad that he had met them and always looked forward to their meetings. Tonight was going to be different, however. Sal had a plan he wanted to share with them to see whether it made sense to them.

"OK, mangiamo," Sal said again.

Ben laughed and said, "You don't have to tell me 'Mangiamo' twice."

Sal loved it. He waited until they had prepared their plates and were sitting around the table.

"I had a rather interesting meeting with Abbey Connors last week," Sal said. "How'd it go?" Buddy asked.

"It was OK. A bit of a rocky start, but all in all, pretty good. Abbey is under a lot of stress. She's covering not only her job but James's and Michael's as well. In Abbey's words, 'Those two shitheads couldn't find their asses in a phone booth.' I also learned that Blue Ridge Vista is going through a second acquisition and reorganization. The first group went bankrupt after COVID, and there were Medicare fraud issues—a real mess. The new owner is EverStar, a private equity group out of Boston. They have established two LLCs: one to operate the health-care facility and the other to own all the land, over eight hundred and fifty acres. Sounds like a real cluster.

"Abbey is a very talented person, and I told her so. She's got a lot on her plate, and she cares about Blue Ridge Vista. I said I would like to keep in touch about what's going on, and she was OK with it.

"What did you think, T, when you talked with James, Michael, and Abbey? Did you notice anything particular in Abbey's behavior or conversation?" asked Sal.

"What do you mean, Sal?" asked T. "I talked with them the day before, and she seemed just fine."

"Did you actually talk with Abbey in the meeting or James and Michael?" Sal asked. "Now that you mention it, James and Michael did all the talking. Abbey just listened and twitched a little while she looked around the room," said T. "Sal, tell us what the heck happened," said Ben.

Sal paused, thinking about the meeting with Abbey, not sure if he wanted to share the entirety of the conversation. He felt the eyes of the Knights pushing him backwards, wanting to understand what he had discovered. Sal slowly began to calmly talk about the meeting.

"Jeez Sal, what the hell," said Buddy, "What happened? "As he put another piece of bread and salami in his mouth. "This is good stuff, Sal. I love it."

"Well, James and Michael were not able to make the meeting that I had scheduled. The receptionist told me that Abbey would be in their place, but she was running late. I figured, no big deal. I could talk with her, and she could tell me if what we were noticing was accurate.

"You know, so I told her about the things we discussed: the painting, the frayed carpet, the clogged gutters, just the general condition of the property and grounds."

"OK," said Ben, "then what?"

"This is where the meeting got a little bumpy."

"How so?" asked Buddy.

"Abbey went into this rant about how she actually ran the show at Blue Ridge Vista and that James and Michael were just a pair of pricks, and if she had a penis she would be in charge."

"Get out," said Ben. "You mean she just started going off like that for no reason? That's unbelievable. I wish I could have been there. I need to go to meetings with you."

"So, you just sat there while this was going on and didn't say anything?" asked T. "Well, maybe I did say something," Sal said.

"What the hell could it have been?" asked Buddy.

"It wasn't my fault. I suggested I might reschedule the meeting when James and Michael could attend. She questioned my insecurity in dealing with a woman, and I said that I couldn't help with the penis thing because I wasn't Dr. Phil or Dr. Laura. I was doing my best at trying not to let her get under my skin."

"What the hell did you say?" asked T.

"My first thought was she might need some new meds, but I didn't say that to her. My next thought was she needed some sex to lighten her attitude, but I didn't say that either."

"Holy shit, Sal," asked Buddy. "What were you thinking? This must have been some meeting."

"Like I said, she started it when she called me an old man, and it went downhill from
there."

"No shit," said Buddy. "You *are* an old man."

"Man, this is great," said Ben. "When are you going to meet with her again? Because I want to go."

"We don't have another meeting planned yet, but all in all, I think we got along pretty well, really. I think she's warming up to me," said Sal.

"Not sure I would agree with your assessment, Sal," said T, "but you certainly have a way about you."

"Well, thank you, T."

"That wasn't really a complement, Sal."

"Just in case it was, I appreciate it."

"The real reason I wanted to talk with you is that I think we need to do some digging and find out just what the hell is going on here. Something is making Abbey act the way she is. I know I may have upset her a bit, but for her to react the way she did tells me something else."

"Maybe it's you," said Ben kiddingly.

Sal walked across the living room and reached into a drawer below the bookshelf and got out a box. Inside were four eighteen-inch hand-carved miniature swords. He placed one in front of each of them. They marveled at the degree of artisanship reflected by the carvings and were silent.

"Sal, these are cool," said Buddy. "And kind of you," added T. "How'd you do this?" asked Ben.

"I had a piece of walnut that I found in the debris from a storm here about a month ago. I took it to the maintenance shop, and they let me borrow their equipment to cut them down to size and shape them. Just a little something to inspire us," Sal said.

"Inspire us?" asked Ben. "Yes," said Sal.

"To do what?" asked Buddy.

"May be a bit silly, but I think Blue Ridge Vista is our king-dom now, and we are the good guys who look out for one another. Like knights. These are symbols of our bond to each other and remind us to protect what we have for ourselves and each other," Sal explained. "We keep these on the table in front of us while we are dealing with the business of our kingdom, like the Knights of the Round Table."

"Wow," said Ben. "Me, a Knight—I never would have guessed."

"That took some real imagination, Sal," said Buddy.

"An interesting thought process," T said.

"So, for each meeting, you go over to the drawer in the living room, next to the bookshelf, and get your sword. OK?"

They all agreed and thought their casual meetings would never be the same. Sal's vision was to be proactive for the benefit of the residents of Blue Ridge Vista, but to do that, the Knights needed to know how the place worked and didn't work.

Sal was open to any ideas about how they could help. For example, how would they know if the place was going down the drain financially?

Ben responded, "Our little jewelry and watch shop had books that recorded all the expenses, liabilities, and cash flow. It would be more complicated and on a much larger scale for Blue Ridge Vista, but the fundamentals would be the same.

"These facilities have cost centers for operation purposes that are charged expenses for the items they use and service. That is the simple explanation for that small portion of this type of business. They receive resident fees that are on the income side."

"Without access to the financials, we are just guessing on the financial viability of Blue Ridge Vista," said T.

"We would need to get the financials and have someone qualified review them and explain them to us," said Buddy.

Ben had an idea. "I met Esther Rudolph the other day at lunch. She was a secretary and treasurer for a large manufacturing company. I'm sure she could tell us if there is something wrong or suspicious in the financials. Why don't two of us take her to lunch off-site and talk to her? We need to explain how sensitive our request is, and it must remain confidential."

"That's a great idea, Ben," said Sal. "Which two of us were you thinking?"

"Why not you and me, as long as you don't talk to Esther like you did to Abbey."

"Funny," said Sal.

T and Buddy agreed that Ben and Sal would be the best ones to talk with Esther. Ben knew her, and Sal could drive them in his truck.

The Knights' first assignment was noted. They would have an update for their meeting next week.

"Now let's finish this food, have some more wine, and get some rest. Tomorrow, we start," Sal said.

Chapter Nine:

SAMMY

De-Lo was making real progress at Blue Ridge Vista. Ruiz regularly kept Judge Carmichael informed and kept Chuck away. His coworkers had complimentary things to say about De-Lo, as he was always willing to help someone out. He liked to work, which was starting to make some of the others who didn't like to work as much look lazy, because they were.

Sammy made it his business to invade De-Lo's space and take him off his stride.

"Hey dog, Sup, what's with the working so hard bullshit, I mean, what the fuck you tryin' to prove?"

De-Lo kept cleaning the floors and moving the furniture to make sure every inch was vacuumed. Sammy cut right into his path one more time and De-Lo hit his foot with the vacuum.

"Ain't you hearin' me bitch, I'm talkin' to you fool, look at me."

De-Lo kept his head down and started to vacuum in a different direction. One more time Sammy got in his grill.

"Hey nigga, you deaf?"

De Lo- turned. "I got work to do, so do you." That pissed Sammy off.

"I ain't goin' repeat myself, mother fucker, you hearin' me."

Ruiz was off in the other corner of the ballroom and noticed Sammy in front of De-Lo. Ruiz had picked up on it on more than one occasion. De-Lo didn't want to complain; he wanted to handle his problem himself, but the fact of the matter was Sammy knew he was getting to De-Lo, and he liked it. It was just a matter before Sammy was going to push De-Lo to his breaking point.

De-Lo decided the next time Sammy interrupted him while he was working, he would get in Sammy's face and settle it, whatever there was to settle. It didn't take long before the confrontation happened.

De-Lo was helping set up tables in the main dining room for a special event to welcome new board members. In the same dining area, Abbey was coordinating the tables, linens, flower arrangements, and more. A brief slide presentation was planned for the local community officials and their spouses, along with some outside guests she had never met, and which was kept quite secret. Abbey had concluded that the secret guests were EverStar execs and possibly other potential investors in Blue Ridge Vista. The event was open to all the residents too. They were expecting over two hundred total attendees.

The day had started early. A public relations firm hired by James set up the video and sound system with large screens in strategic places for everyone in the audience to have an unrestricted view of the presentation. Abbey was in her element, even though she knew nothing about the outside group, and it was driving her crazy.

The Knights would be in attendance because all the residents had received invitations to meet the new EverStar board members. Sal and Ben decided to walk over to the common area for a sneak preview of the venue. From a distance, Sal could see Abbey and pointed her out to Ben.

"I need to meet that lady," Ben said with a loud laugh.

"Not now," said Sal, trying to push him along, only to see De-Lo talking with a guy and trying to get out of the guy's way.

Sal could see he was agitated and waited for De-Lo to move to a different area in the large dining room to help with the chairs.

Sal said, "Hey, Ben, pardon me; I'll be right back."

Sal moved in the direction of Sammy and nonchalantly slid close enough to introduce himself and let him know that De-Lo was his friend.

"What are you doing, old man?" Sammy said.

Sal thought, *this is not a great start to introductions.* He was the second person to call him an old man, but what the heck? He paused and answered, "I'm looking at a guy who is bothering my friend De-Lo."

"Get your ass out of my face before I kick it back to your old lady," Sammy said.

Sal took a deep breath and paused again. "You're going to kick my ass and brag to your homies about beating up a seventy-six-year-old guy? You can't be the smartest in your family," Sal said.

"I'm going to knock your ass into next week, you prick. Now how do you like that?"

"Look, I can see we got off on the wrong foot. De-Lo is my friend, and he's working on a new beginning, and he doesn't need the trouble you're selling. Keep out of his space, got it?"

"What you gonna do, pops? Beat me up?" Sammy laughed in Sal's face.

"No, I wouldn't think of that. I'm a pacifist," said Sal.

"What the fuck is that fool?" was the next thing out of Sammy's mouth.

"Well, let me see if I can explain it to you in a way you can understand. This is going to be a challenge, so follow me.

"Pacifists don't like violence at all, no way. They just can't stand the thought of it. It makes them sick," Sal said.

"So?" said Sammy.

"I just want you to leave De-Lo to himself; don't bother him and let him do his work, OK?"

"Or what?" Sammy said.

"Look, we got off on the wrong foot, but I can promise you one thing. You're not going to like what might happen to you if you keep bothering him, got it?"

Sal leaned in a little closer to Sammy and extended his hand as a gesture of peace while Sammy did the same, smiling with a bit of arrogance.

Sal gripped Sammy's hand and squeezed hard. His short fingers belied his hand strength, and Sammy was finding that out now. Sal increased the pressure.

"I need you and me to have what they call 'an understanding.' Do you know what an understanding is, Sammy?"

Now Sammy was breathing hard and wincing in pain. He nodded to Sal as sweat was pouring from his head and face.

"OK then, we have an understanding. I'm glad we could have this talk," Sal said. "You ever, ever going to bother De-Lo, ever even going to look at him?"

Sammy just shook his head, his lips quivering. "You be safe out there. Be careful, OK?" said Sal.

"You might want to get cleaned up. I think you had an accident—at least it smells like it," Sal said as he tapped Sammy on the shoulder, "*Capiche paisano?*"

Sammy stayed bent over for about ten minutes, taking deep breaths and looking around to see if anyone had seen what had just happened as Sal casually strolled out of the room.

Chapter Ten:

THE SEARCH COMMITTEE

Sal looked for Ben to see what he thought about the setup for the main event. He said it looked good, but he wanted to meet Abbey.

There was more work to do, like schedule lunch with Esther.

Ben suggested that the lunch date could be the next day. It sounded good to Sal.

Sal let T and Buddy know that they were going out to lunch tomorrow and asked them to share any ideas they had on how to broach the subject of Blue Ridge Vista finances with Esther. Ben and Sal were going to do their best to solicit Esther's help and expertise and confidence.

Ben picked the perfect place: outdoor dining, a nice table by the fountain, and a great view of the town. The menu was elderly friendly: easy to read, simple, and moderately priced.

To make sure there would be no issue when the check arrived, Sal asked the waiter to give him the check before anyone ordered.

"Can I offer you any beverages? We have summer tea, naked Hawaiian Punch, and other soft drinks," the waiter said.

"What about adult beverages?" Sal asked. "Esther, would you like anything in the adult beverage section?"

"Well, that sounds great. I would like a glass of pinot grigio, please," Esther said. "Wonderful," Sal said. "How about you, Ben?"

"I think I'll try a chardonnay."

"Splendid," Sal responded. "And I'll have a Peroni."

"I'll have that for you shortly," replied the server.

"Esther, how long have you been at Blue Ridge?" Sal asked. "About four years. It's a nice place," she said.

I agree," said Ben. "Both Sal and I are relatively new arrivals. I was here before Sal but not by much—we're coming up on four and five months," he said.

"Esther, before Blue Ridge Vista, where was home for you?" Ben asked. "A small town in southern Indiana," she replied.

"No kidding—get out," Ben said with a smile. "I'm from Terre Haute, Indiana. What a small world. My parents fled Romania in the nineteen forties to escape persecution from the Nazis. We lived in Terre Haute for over forty years."

"That must have been an unbelievable journey for your family. I can't even begin to imagine," said Esther.

"To be honest, my family always would remind me of their trek to America and how thankful they were to live here. We loved every moment of living in Indiana. It is a beautiful state with beautiful people."

"How do you like Blue Ridge Vista, Esther?" asked Sal.

"Oh, it's beautiful. Nice people, well managed; used to be better, but they do a pretty good job."

"I'm curious, what do you mean by 'used to be better'?" Sal asked.

"Oh, you know, the little things: the outside shrubs, the weeds, the paint—just stuff like that."

Ben perked up, as did Sal.

"You know, Esther," Ben said, "Sal and I have noticed the same things since we've been here."

"Yes, for me it started a little over a year ago. Blue Ridge Vista had a change in the office.

James was first, and then Michael showed up. Abbey was the last one. She got here about six or seven months ago. I can't be certain, but it was around that time."

"Wow," said Ben. "We appreciate you sharing that with us. We were wondering if it was only us who noticed the things you mentioned."

Ben was doing great, and Sal just listened.

"Esther, I must be honest with you. Sal and I have been noticing some other things as well. Sal had a meeting with Abbey last week that didn't go so well. The details aren't important unless Sal would like to be more specific."

"Now you've piqued my curiosity," said Esther.

"Oh, it was nothing at all, Esther, just a minor difference of opinion," said Sal. "Well, how'd she take it?" asked Esther, almost knowing Ben's answer. "Better than expected," said Sal.

"Are you kidding me?" said Ben. "Abbey went off the rails; she went crazy on you. My God, Sal, I was really surprised that you kept your composure, really." Ben just laughed some more.

"I've got to hear this," said Esther. "I could use a good story, and don't leave out any of the details."

"Let's just leave it at that for now," Sal said. "We'll save it for when we have more time. Promise."

Ben explained what he, Sal, T, and Buddy were trying to do. He also said how much they needed and would appreciate Esther's corporate financial knowledge to confirm their suspicions.

After listening to Ben, Esther calmly briefed the two on corporate finance, the uniqueness of different types of enterprises, and the common basics, regardless of structure.

Ben and Sal got an unbelievable lesson. Esther shared her expertise for ten to fifteen minutes, but in the end, she said, "The only way to confirm what you suspect would be to review the Blue Ridge Vista financials, which would not be possible."

Ben was amazed. Esther had a wealth of knowledge and had reached the same conclusion that the Knights had suggested at their last round table discussion.

Sal and Ben wondered what was next. "Esther, how could we get them?" asked Ben.

"I am quite sure they are stored on James's and Michael's hard drives," she replied. "I know they won't give them to you."

"Suppose we could get them—would you review them and let us know your opinion?"

"Sure, I would, and then you can tell me the rest of the story about Abbey. Agreed?"

Sal shook his head, looked at Ben, and just smiled. How could they ever get the financials of Blue Ridge? That would be the round table topic of discussion next Monday night. Until then, Ben and Sal would do a debrief after lunch to make sure they were on the same page.

The ride back from lunch gave them more time to talk and visit with Esther, and they both enjoyed her company.

Chapter Eleven:

ROUND TABLE II

S al was prepping the food and wine for the Knights' meeting. They had a lot of ground to cover following their lunch with Esther. She had basically come to the same conclusions that Ben and Sal had discussed a week ago.

Sal was wondering how they could possibly get the financials to confirm what they suspected.

T and Buddy arrived five minutes early. T reached into the drawer Sal had shown them and opened the box of cloth-wrapped swords.

"Holy shit," T said. He never swore; it must've been Sal's bad influence. "What's the matter?" asked Buddy.

"You've gotta see this." T brought the swords to the table.

"Good lord," said Buddy. "These are beautiful. When did you do this, Sal?"

"I didn't do this! Look at how beautiful these are. Our monograms, the gold band, the stones—each one different. Unbelievable," said Sal.

Just about then, Ben walked in.

"Sorry I'm late. I was visiting with Esther and talking about the nice time we had at lunch. Who would have guessed we both have roots in Indiana? Small world, don't you think?" he said.

"Ben, did you do this?" T asked. "Do what?" Ben replied.

"These swords: they have our initials monogrammed on a gold band. And these birthstones—how in the world? How did you figure out our birth months, or did you just guess?" asked Buddy.

"I have my ways of discovery." Ben laughed in his patented way. "Yeah, I did that over the weekend. I got them when Sal took a walk, worked on them for two days, and put them back before he noticed they were gone."

"These are beautiful. Thank you. You did way too much here. These had to be expensive," said T.

"In case you want to know, Buddy's was the most expensive because he was born in April. The diamond is his birthstone."

"I never knew I had a birthstone, Ben," said Sal. "You are amazing."

"I have my moments," Ben said with a sound that started in his stomach before making its way to his mouth, followed by his perfect smile. "If we are the Knights, we need a little bling, don't you think?"

"C'mon, let's get started," said Sal.

Sal, T, and Buddy just stared at Ben as he made his way to his chair.

Ben and Sal shared everything about their lunch meeting with Esther and the fact that she had noticed the same things that were bothering them. The financials would provide the proof to confirm their suspicions about the run-down condition of the paint, the carpet, the landscaping, and just the general property maintenance. Where were the monies being spent or diverted?

"Any ideas?" Sal asked.

"Maybe there is a way to piece this puzzle together," said T. "What do you mean?" said Buddy.

T explained that the guys knew the supervisors in the maintenance and food service sections of Blue Ridge Vista. Maybe there was a way to see if their budgets and expenditures had changed by a large amount over the last year or so. Also, they could review the resident roster to see whether there was an increase or decrease affecting the income stream.

"Smart," commented Sal. He suggested that each of them focus on a separate section at Blue Ridge Vista and test their theory. They would start the next day and have their findings for next week's meeting.

Sal said he would talk to Ruiz to explain their theory. Like other conversations, this would be confidential. Ben would check food service, and Buddy would schmooze the lady who oversaw the resident role. T would work another angle through some of his former colleagues in his old firm.

Chapter Twelve:

THE DE-LO ZONE

Judge Carmichael was receiving regular updates from Ruiz, having bypassed Chuck's probation authority. It was working much better that way. Ruiz was so impressed by De-Lo's work that during his last conversation with Judge Carmichael, he suggested a new challenge on the inside of Blue Ridge Vista.

Ruiz confided in the judge that De-Lo had gained tremendous confidence with each new assignment, and he was convinced he could handle additional responsibilities. He shared with the judge that all the monitoring proved he was making progress, and with the judge's permission, he suggested removing his ankle transmitter.

Judge Carmichael said he wanted to take that into consideration, and he would give Ruiz an answer next week. Ruiz would continue to mentor De-Lo to succeed, knowing that he appreciated his counsel and friendship.

In the back of his mind, Ruiz was convinced that De-Lo could handle much more challenging tasks. His high school transcripts, while not complete, indicated an intelligent young man who had made some bad choices. Unfortunately, Ruiz had seen far too many De-Los in his lifetime, but this was one he knew he could help.

Ruiz shared with De-Lo the conversation that he had had with Judge Carmichael. While he couldn't promise anything, Ruiz wanted De-Lo to know he had at least two guys in his corner trying to help.

De-Lo smiled in a way he hadn't in a long time. It was a bit unusual, and it felt good. He decided that whatever it took, he was not going to screw this up. Sammy was no longer in his face. It was almost as if he was afraid of De-Lo, and he didn't care. He only wanted to be left alone to do his work. De-Lo was happy with the good decisions he was making.

Ruiz and Judge Carmichael talked on a somewhat regular basis. Ruiz would share De-Lo's progress. They both had an investment in how De-Lo was adjusting to his new temporary home. Judge Carmichael's interest was both professional and admittedly personal in nature, as his reputation was on the line. He had used his judicial discretion to make De-Lo's placement at Blue Ridge Vista something he owned, and he did.

Whatever his next assignment, De-Lo knew he could handle it. Confidence is an amazing medicine, and De-Lo was gaining more daily. His grandmother Rose would be so proud of what he was doing and how he was maturing.

The judge gave permission for De-Lo to visit Rose the next weekend. Sal offered to drive him, and the judge approved the request. They would leave for DC in the morning. De-Lo could barely sleep; this would be his first time away from Blue Ridge Vista in four months. He couldn't wait until morning.

Sal picked up De-Lo at 8:30 a.m., and they grabbed some breakfast before they hit the road. DC was about a forty-five-minute drive from Blue Ridge Vista. It gave Sal and De-Lo some time to catch up on things.

This was a new guy compared to the one he had initially met, Sal thought. He was smiling and engaging and quite a conversationalist. Sal was proud, and so was De-Lo, who shared that the guy who had been bothering him quit coming around.

"I'm glad to hear that," said Sal. "What else is going on?"

"If all goes well, I will get my ankle monitor off next week. What a relief that will be," De-Lo said.

"That's great news. I'm proud of you," Sal replied.

"The judge and Ruiz have been overseeing my probation instead of Chuck, and that's been a huge blessing," De-Lo said. "I might have a new assignment next week on the inside of Blue Ridge Vista, possibly in a training-level job. How cool is that?"

"That's huge," said Sal. "Wait until your grandmother hears the good news. I know she'll be proud of all the work you've done and the progress you've made."

They were about five minutes away from De-Lo's grandmother's apartment. He was getting understandably excited, even though he was nineteen years old. He loved Grandmother Rose. She had saved his life.

"Well, here we are," said De-Lo. "I can get out right here. Do you want to come in and meet my grandma?" De-Lo asked.

"All due respect, De-Lo, you've earned this time, and I want you to enjoy every minute.

Take your time, and I'll see you tomorrow. What time would you like me to pick you up?"

"How about noon? That way I can go to church and take her to breakfast, OK?"

"Sounds like a perfect plan. See you tomorrow."

"Thanks so much, Sal."

"Enjoy yourself, De-Lo. You've earned it."

Chapter Thirteen:

T'S TRUTH

Sal had mixed feelings of anxiety and anticipation on his drive back to Blue Ridge Vista. Thinking of De-Lo's visit with his grandmother and all the progress he was making was remarkable. Sal was trying to help De-Lo and at the same time work with the Knights to confirm their suspicion about the way Blue Ridge Vista was being mismanaged. After all, this was their home, and they seemed confident something was going to jeopardize the entire community.

They would all be anxious to see what intel they had gathered from the different departments at Blue Ridge Vista.

Sal was going to get something to eat and a good night's sleep. He could go for a longer walk in the morning. He would see whether Ben, T, or Buddy might be interested in joining him.

Sal woke up at 6:00 a.m. So much for sleeping in. Nothing would change; he had been waking up at 6:00 a.m. over the last fifty-plus years. He got the newspaper and had a cup of coffee out on his patio. He could see Ben headed his way; it was 7:30 a.m.

"There's a pot of coffee on; help yourself," Sal said. He could see Buddy and T right behind Ben. They all had some coffee, hit the john, and were on their way. Blue Ridge Vista was peaceful in the mornings; there was no traffic noise, only the sounds of the birds and sprinklers on Sundays. It was perfect.

"Which direction do you want to go today, Ben?" Buddy asked. "Not sure; hadn't thought about it. How about you, T?"

"Let's flip a coin," T suggested. "Call it in the air, Ben," said T. "Heads," said Ben.

"Heads it is. Which way are we headed?" asked T.

Ben pointed in a direction they hadn't been to before, slightly downhill, to the southeast of the Blue Ridge Vista pavilion.

"Grab some water, and let's get going," said Sal. "I have to be back by ten thirty to go get De-Lo at his grandmother's."

Ben was in the front, the leader of the pack. These were cool times for the Knights, giving them a chance to learn more about one another and their families and help their community at the same time. They were much at ease.

T shared something no one could have imagined. His retirement from the Kauffman Firm had been a contentious split with the firm his father had founded. As T's duties had dramatically increased in the practice, he now had younger staff completing tasks that he had once normally done himself. Drafting contracts for real estate transactions, reviewing corporate bylaws, and approving the agenda for board meetings now became the day-to-day duties of new and talented staff. Senior members of the firm reviewed this work, but normally as a cursory task. T did not handle the complete transaction on the Blue Ridge Vista property, and he thought it next to impossible that EverStar Equity could pull the deal off in thirty days. He was right, as he later discovered.

On the rare occasion that he did make a trip with his family and unbeknownst to him, all the closing docs, complete with environmental reports, were shared with EverStar. T would only learn of this some five years after the sale and never knew the name of the partner who completed it. As part of the closing terms and conditions, EverStar imposed a separate confidentiality agreement on the Kaufman firm. This transaction remained confidential. The firm received a bonus of over $1 million in addition to their $1 million fee.

What T had feared had happened. The firm's political and financial clout had grown to a new level and exposed the ugly truth. Attorneys with greedy financial visions, while rationalized as somehow altruistic by the amount of pro bono work and charities they fund, believe they are special in a different way.

EverStar had several high-level politicians in its pocket. One was chair of the Senate Banking Committee, one was a congressman from a highly influential area of New York City, another was chair of the House Finance Committee, and another was a cabinet member, the secretary of transportation. The congressmen were not of the same political party, just to confirm that greed is not owned by any one group in Washington, DC.

They had spent years in politics amassing phenomenal financial wealth and influence that they never could have earned in the private sector, and each had easily won reelection. The new secretary of transportation, a real phony who thought he was the smartest guy in the room, was in favor of the project. He cited the creation of new, well-paying jobs as part of the infrastructure bill, which was aided by unspent COVID-19 funds from the three years prior. He was traveling the states of Maryland and Virginia, touting the bipartisan effort to do what was best for the local economy. The news media and Sunday-morning shows loved it.

The project in question was a highway bypass to connect an interstate right outside Washington, DC. It would save drivers a twenty-minute drive to the Blue Ridge Vista Senior Living

Community. Blue Ridge Vista would have its own exit as part of the plan.

The problem for Blue Ridge: about two hundred residents were going to be relocated because of a forced bankruptcy that was about to occur. They just didn't know it.

"I realize that this is all my fault. I apologize to you, my true friends. I will do anything I can to expose those in my old firm and the politicians who are in the pockets of EverStar. I'm just not sure how we can do it," T said.

Chapter Fourteen:

PLAYING POKER

The next meeting of the roundtable was the most focused of all their gatherings. Ben, Sal, and Buddy had done their homework, having talked with key supervisors about their suspicions and desire to fix the problem. The question was, how were they going to do it?

Ben listened intently as the information about department spending, supplies, services, and the loss of residents, combined with the work stoppage on any new patio homes, was discussed. The downward trends in Blue Ridge Vista numbers could be an anomaly.

"Suppose we tell James and Michael that we have information that we plan to share with the state attorney general on intentional financial mismanagement at Blue Ridge Vista," Ben said.

"What?" said Buddy. "How can we prove that?"

"We don't have to," said Ben. "We just tell them and see how they react."

"You know, it's like we're playing poker," said Buddy.

"But what happens if they call our bluff?" asked Sal.

"Personally, I don't think they would want that kind of negative publicity," said Ben. "How would that look for Blue Ridge

Vista, EverStar and the politicians? I don't think that's a bet they want to take," said T.

"Man, that's unbelievably risky," said Buddy. "But it's sure worth a shot. What do you guys think?"

"This is way above my pay grade," said Sal. "Let's walk through how you think we can do it and what the conversation with James and Michael is going to sound like."

"I think we have to keep working to gather more information to support our theory," said Buddy. "But this sure is a good plan. Well done, Ben."

"Salud," said Sal as he raised a glass of wine to honor the work they all had done and Ben's idea to flush out the bad guys.

Over the next two weeks, the Knights would keep to the plan. Ben would talk with Esther and let her know what they were planning. She might have some more thoughts on how to gather any type of financial information.

The nursing and senior care units of Blue Ridge Vista had to file certain reports with federal agencies, as well as state and local. Esther's computer skills would be very helpful in gathering any public information.

T was going to reach out to one of his few contacts at his old firm to see if anything else regarding Everstar had recently surfaced about Blue Ridge Vista.

Buddy was going to inquire about the construction delay and see when he would be able to start selling patio homes again.

Sal was going to talk with Ruiz to see if he had heard anything that might help the Knights get leverage.

That was about the best plan the Knights had now, it wasn't much but it was better than nothing.

Chapter Fifteen:

De-Lo's Pain

On Sal's way back to pick up De-Lo, he was imagining the time De-Lo had with his grandmother and how proud she must be. He was also a bit preoccupied with the work they had done to expose the mess at Blue Ridge Vista that was flying under the radar.

What if they call their bluff? What would they do? Would they have to leave their new home? So many questions and more were on his mind.

He could see De-Lo right where he had dropped him off. De-Lo was expressionless when Sal stopped.

"You OK, friend? What's up? How was your time with your grandma?" Sal asked.

De-Lo barely had enough energy to open the door, and he stared straight ahead, not acknowledging Sal's questions at all. He covered his face and began to cry and cry. Sal pulled the truck off into a parking lot to try to console De-Lo any way he could.

"It's my grandma," he said. "She has terminal cancer. Six weeks to live, according to her doctor."

"De-Lo, I'm so sorry. What can I do for you? Please, tell me."

"I don't know; I have no idea. This isn't fair. She's the best person in the whole world.

She raised me when my own mom couldn't. Oh, God, please help my grandma, and help me help her," De-Lo said.

Sal was silent. He didn't know what he could do for his friend, but he wanted to do something. They sat together for a while, and Sal listened. He was heartsick for De-Lo but could only imagine how upside-down his world had just gotten.

"What would you like to do?" Sal asked. "You want to stay here? I can try to reach Judge Carmichael and let him know what you just found out. I'll be glad to help you any way I can."

"You know, Sal, I believe you, and that means a lot to me. You and the other guys at Blue Ridge Vista have helped me in so many ways. I appreciate it. I just need to figure this out myself; at least I have to try."

"OK," said Sal. "But please let us know. I don't want to bug you, only help you."

"Thanks again," De-Lo said.

The drive home was tremendously quiet and sad. As if De-Lo didn't have enough on his plate—doing his best, making real progress, working into a quasi-office and team member—before he had this dropped on him.

Five minutes away from Blue Ridge Vista, Sal asked De-Lo to consider his offer, that if he needed anything—a ride, some money, some advice, someone to listen to—just say the word.

De-Lo headed to his room at Blue Ridge Vista. Sal headed back to his place, his mind wandering about the pain De-Lo must be feeling. . De-Lo was maturing, gaining confidence and responsibility. Rose's diagnosis would be another setback for him, but his support system at Blue Ridge Vista was going to embrace him, and De-Lo knew it.

Sal decided to stop at Ben's house to tell him about De-Lo's grandmother. Ben was speechless. They talked briefly and decided to go to T's and Buddy's to let them know about De-Lo. It was a very slow walk.

T and Buddy listened to everything Sal mentioned. T suggested that the guys reach out to Ruiz and Judge Carmichael to keep them informed, they were both stakeholders in De-Lo's world. T suggested that out of respect for De-Lo's privacy, the fewer people who knew, the better. But they all asked the same question: What could they do? Ben suggested following De-Lo's lead, hoping he would be open to any way that they could help him with money, travel, going with him to see his grandmother—anything.

They all thought the next week would be tough, and they were right. T called Judge Carmichael for some advice. The judge told them that he trusted their judgment regarding

De-Lo, as the judge could see the progress he had been making. The judge asked them to notify him in advance as they made their plans to help De-Lo. They all agreed.

The Knights had a more immediate problem to deal with than Blue Ridge Vista. A young man and good friend needed their help and support. De-Lo was the age of their grandchildren, and Rose was their age. This placed his pain in a totally different light.

Buddy had an idea.

"Hey, what if we could pay for De-Lo's grandma to live here at Blue Ridge Vista, in a private room in the assisted living section? That way he could see her every day and spend as much time as he needed to make her comfortable. We get the judge's blessing, ask Ruiz to give him the time, and we cover the cost?"

They all thought that sounded great, but they would need to get it cleared by James Dillon, the executive director, before they could tell De-Lo their idea. If this worked, it would surely ease some of his pain. They were starting to think like a family.

They thought it would be best if they all went together to meet with James to make the request.

T offered to call first thing in the morning to get the appointment for the same day.

They sat around sharing stories as they had in the past, only this time they struggled to find anything other than De-Lo and his grandmother to talk about. He had made such an impression on these guys in such a short time. Why did this have to happen to his grandma, and to him?

The Knights were at the Blue Ridge Vista executive offices by 9:00 a.m. the following morning. T had prepared in advance what he was going to say to James, just as he had prepared for negotiations in the past. This time, however, his thought process existed in a different zone. He had made this personal.

The receptionist greeted T. "Please accept my apology Mr. Kaufman, I was just informed that Mr. Dillon has an emergency staff meeting and he won't be able to meet with you this morning. I was asked to reschedule your meeting sometime within the next two weeks.".

Out of nowhere, T said, "Tell him to change his plans, now."

Ben, Sal, and Buddy were shocked—this was a T they had never seen.

The receptionist said, "Mr. Dillon told me to tell you that is out of the question." What happened next absolutely blew Sal, Ben, and Buddy's minds.

T got up, walked past the receptionist, and into James's office, closing the door behind him. The others were trying to imagine the conversation. Sal said he wished he could be in there to hone some of his negotiating skills. Ben told Sal that he didn't have those skills. Buddy was just watching and listening and enjoying every minute.

Fifteen minutes later, T walked out, looked at the guys, and said, "We're done here. Let's go."

The guys looked at one another as T walked out, and they followed, not knowing anything.

They weren't outside the main entrance before Sal asked, "What the hell did you say to James, T? I mean, what the hell just happened?"

T kept walking, his stride slowing as he turned to the three of them and said that De-Lo's grandmother would be moving to Blue Ridge Vista tomorrow. She would have a private room, De-Lo could stay with her if he liked, and Blue Ridge Vista was going to comp all the costs associated with her care out of their generosity. They would arrange for Rose's transportation from her apartment to Blue Ridge Vista, and her room would be ready tomorrow.

"What the heck?" said Ben. "How in the world? You are the man, T. This is great for Rose and De-Lo."

Sal was so impressed by T, and he told him so. Buddy just smiled because he knew T had worked some real magic, the kind that he wished he could do.

As they walked down the circular drive to the entrance of Blue Ridge Vista, nobody said anything. T was in front, walking at a deliberate pace; no one was beside him, only behind. Buddy, Sal, and Ben were staring at T and admiring what had just happened. How in the hell would a senior living community comp hospice care twenty-four-seven? *T must have some huge cajones,* was all Sal was thinking, *to be able to force Blue Ridge Vista to do this.* T knew something more than the rest of them.

They stopped before going to their homes to discuss telling De-Lo the news. As a group, they thought that T should be the one to tell De-Lo since he had negotiated the deal. "Negotiate" was probably a stretch, but T had gotten Blue Ridge Vista to agree with the idea in total.

"T, how about you tell De-Lo what Blue Ridge Vista is offering to do for his grandmother?" said Buddy.

"Maybe it would be better if Sal told him, "said T.

"With all due respect, T, you got this done, and it would be better coming from you," Sal said, and Ben and Buddy nodded in agreement.

T thought for a moment, a little nervous, considering he had never done anything like this before. He would have never considered doing something like threatening somebody, but he felt good doing it for a young guy who needed a break.

He agreed to tell De-Lo the news. T walked over to the facilities office and asked De-Lo's supervisor if he could have a word with him. The supervisor told T that he could use his office to talk with him. T thanked him and waited until De-Lo walked in.

"Good afternoon, De-Lo. You got a minute?" T closed the door and told De-Lo that arrangements were made at Blue Ridge Vista for his grandmother to be transferred there, if that was all right with him.

De-Lo was stunned, cupped his hands to his face, and began to cry. He was overwhelmed, not having any idea how he could afford this for his grandmother.

"De-Lo, the arrangements are covered by Blue Ridge—all of them. Let's keep this confidential, OK?"

"Absolutely, but how?"

"Not to worry, friend. I am just glad this worked out and you can have some time to spend with your grandmother."

"Thank you, Mr. Kaufman."

"Please call me T."

They walked out of the office in different directions. T knew that Ruiz was going to talk to De-Lo about taking as much time as he needed to be with his grandmother.

For once in his life, De-Lo had people who were helping him, and he didn't know why.

He couldn't explain it, but it made him feel safe and loved, something like being with his grandmother.

Chapter Sixteen:

ROUND TABLE III

The last two weeks had been an emotional and reflective challenge for the Knights. With the news of De-Lo's grandmother and T's sharing about his departure from his law firm and confronting the executive team at Blue Ridge Vista, the Knights had a lot on their plate. At this round table meeting, they would take some time to digest the past week's happenings and plan their next strategy to help De-Lo and dig more into the real EverStar plan for Blue Ridge Vista.

Buddy opened the drawer in the living room to get the swords for the meeting and placed them in front of each of the chairs. Sal finished the salami and cheese board, placing the marinated olives and roasted red peppers and fresh Italian bread on a separate plate. Ben got the small jars for the wine, and T brought his notes to share with the group.

They were all seated, and Sal had filled their glasses. Buddy said, "Salud! To your health!

You know, I really like the way that sounds."

"Mangiamo," Ben replied.

"You guys are the best," T said.

"*Beve*, drink!" Sal said and smiled. He loved this time. He just wished things were different for De-Lo. If only De-Lo had some friends his age to hang with and talk with, someone other than the Knights, it might be easier for him to cope with his grandmother's health and Blue Ridge Vista.

"First thing," Ben said to start the meeting. "Has anyone talked to De-Lo today to see how his grandma is getting along in her new surroundings?"

"I did," said Buddy. "He said she was comfortable and glad to be closer to De-Lo."

"T, you are a magician," said Ben.

"I totally agree," said Sal.

"I told De-Lo to let us know if there is anything he needs. He said that Ruiz told him to take the time he needs to be with Rose," said Buddy.

"We are lucky to have Ruiz in De-Lo's corner," said T.

"OK," said T. "This is what I learned from one of my contacts at the law firm. EverStar is planning an announcement in the next six to eight weeks to present their ideas for Blue Ridge Vista. They are going to have a big national and local media event including the politicians they own and the contractors who will be doing the project. EverStar also intends to have the major golf equipment companies and the pros they sponsor on the tour. It is really going to be something.

"A date hasn't been decided because they still have some documents they need to execute before the announcement. But for all intents and purposes, this is a done deal, I am sad to report."

"Holy crap," said Ben.

"C'mon, guys," said Buddy. "We can figure this out. We're the Knights. We can't just roll over and let these pricks win. What about exposing the evidence we have like we said we would?"

"Buddy, I hear you," said T. "But what we have now is not enough. It would be easy for James and Michael to say we were a bunch of old guys who were making things up. We do have enough to make them squirm, but that's about all at this point."

"We're not going to just give up," said Sal. "Let's keep working on something we haven't thought of yet, OK?"

"Absolutely," said Ben. "Why don't we go for a long walk tomorrow? We'll have the night to get some rest, and things will look better in the morning, OK? What do you say we meet at nine a.m. for our walk. Make sure you have some comfortable shoes and bring some water."

"Where in the heck do you plan on taking us?" said Sal, laughing.

"Not sure just yet," said Ben. "I just thought it would be good to explore this property a bit more. It's a beautiful place that those EverStar assholes want to tear up. Just want to see more than we have."

"Great idea," said Buddy. "But let's finish this food that Sal has prepared. I could eat this every day, Sal."

"Glad you like it, Buddy."

"I love it," said Buddy. "Me too," said T.

"The weather is supposed to be great tomorrow: not too hot, just perfect. Wear comfortable clothes too," said Ben.

"OK, OK, we got it," said Buddy.

Chapter Seventeen:

THE GREAT ADVENTURE

Sal and T got up a little early just to check in with De-Lo to see whether there was anything he needed before they met Ben and Buddy. He said he was fine and that he and his grandma could never thank them enough for their kindness. De-Lo said he was going to make it up to them all, somehow.

T told De-Lo not to think about anything other than keeping his grandma comfortable and to let them know how they could help in any way.

They went to meet Ben and Buddy. Sal was thinking about heading southeast out of Blue Ridge Vista. Buddy had told Ruiz they would be out for a long walk, in case anybody complained about seeing some old guys walking about like they were lost.

Ben said, "I don't give a shit if someone complains about us. We're on a nature walk."

"I like that," said T. "That's exactly what we're doing."

They were about a thousand yards from the main courtyard at Blue Ridge Vista, where there was a slight grade. The Blue Ridge Vista property was spectacular, with huge oak and walnut tress sporadically located on the 850-acre tract, providing beautiful shade and homes for wildlife. It was easy to imagine the property as a pasture: gently rolling hills, maybe a five-foot decline—nothing too dramatic—into a gathering of trees. It somewhat resembled an old orchard but was now overgrown. They had never wandered this far from the main part of the Blue Ridge Vista pavilion.

In the gathering, it appeared that two of the trees had fallen on what looked like a structure of some type. Sal thought it would be neat to look farther into the area of the downed trees. Ben, Buddy, and T told him to be careful because they didn't know anyone else who could fix the antipasto for the next round table. Sal just laughed. Ben walked up to the edge with Sal. There was something beneath the group of trees; Ben could see it much better now.

"What do you think it is, Sal?" he asked.

"Not quite sure, but I want to find out," Sal said.

By now, they had been gone for over two hours. The water they had taken with them was gone, and they were getting hungry and tired. The walking up and down the hills was a bit more than they were used to. Sal had an idea.

"What if we go back, and I will ask Ruiz if we can borrow one of their utility vehicles tomorrow to take a better look at the property? We can ask for a couple of tools, goggles, a saw and ax, and even some rope.

"We'll let him know we were curious about the location down by the old orchard and see what he says. Sound good to you guys?"

They thought for a moment, and all agreed that it sounded like a plan. They weren't quite sure what to expect or what Sal thought he saw in the fallen trees, but what the heck?

They agreed to head back, get some lunch and some rest, and have dinner to talk about the lingering EverStar plot. A nap would be good for all of them.

T wanted to make some calls to follow up on who at his old firm was responsible for the EverStar deal and the debacle that had followed him as he left the practice. Buddy wanted to see what the holdup was on the construction of the planned patio homes. He was getting a commission on each sale as a part of the deal he had cut with Blue Ridge Vista to offset some of the expenses of his home. Plus, to be honest, he loved to sell, and he was good at it.

Ben had a chance to sit down with De-Lo over a soft drink and catch up with him. De-Lo explained that things, while scary for his grandmother, were at least easier for him to deal with daily. Ruiz had been more than generous with him about taking time during the day just to check in with his grandmother. He ate all his meals, every day, with her. He was so thankful that he was able to spend what time she had left with her and just talk about how he grew up and what had happened to his mother.

De-Lo, Ruiz learned, was working overtime each day to make up for the time he spent with his grandmother. Ruiz did not expect De-Lo to do that but shared his work commitment with Judge Carmichael as a testament to the young man's character. For some reason, both Ruiz and the judge were not surprised by his maturity. Rose, after all, had done a remarkable job of raising him in extremely challenging circumstances.

De-Lo had used his time to reflect and confirm some of the pieces of his early childhood life. His grandmother never made excuses for how they lived their lives, but she regretted that De-Lo did not have a responsible male role model in his life. What a difference that would have made. But Rose could see that De-Lo had the loving heart that his mother had before the drugs ruined her life. Rose had promised herself that she would not let De-Lo go down that same path. That was the reason she had worked two jobs all those years: to be an example and to pay the bills for what few extra things she could take care of for him.

De-Lo was learning so much from the meals they were having each day. Rose asked him to read Bible verses that were special to her and would become more special to him. He would read, and then they would discuss what the meaning of God's Word was. De-Lo was surprised by his grandma's understanding of the scripture, and God's Word was seen in the lives they lived.

Rose was charitable even without having money and generous with what she did for others.

De-Lo listened to her explanations, focusing on every word and every lesson. His grandma was a smart and loving woman, he knew that for sure. He remembered her favorite saying: "It's not what you have; it's what you do with what you have." He loved to hear her say that and watch for his expression as she would gently smile.

Each time he left her room, he was comforted and calm, which surprised him. He was so afraid of how he was going to be able to live without his grandmother, and he told her so. He wanted her to know how much he loved and respected everything she had done for him.

Rose told him that he would be fine because he had made some new friends at Blue Ridge Vista. De-Lo had talked with Rose about each of them and how they made him laugh at some of the things that they had done and said.

Rose knew that Sal had driven De-Lo to see her the week before. She knew that T had been able to arrange her being moved to Blue Ridge Vista for better care and to be closer to her grandson. De-Lo had shared all of this with her. De-Lo also told her about Ruiz and Judge Carmichael and how they had both told De-Lo to take as much time as he wanted to spend with his grandmother. In a short time, De-Lo had a network of real support and love. Rose knew this too, and she could sense that De-Lo felt secure with these people. That was Rose's best medicine now.

Chapter Eighteen:

The EverStar Move

The private equity business is a high-risk, high-reward venture for firms other than EverStar. EverStar's strategy was to use all its corporate and political clout to eliminate any risk.

The Blue Ridge Vista property would be a high-end, gated community with an eighteen-hole championship golf club only twenty minutes from Washington, DC. EverStar had already secured a Fortune 500 corporate sponsor for a major tournament that they were waiting to announce at their gala event. The Department of Transportation, in conjunction with the US House and Senate, was in full support of the project. The political contributions and donations, in the millions, were the insurance premium EverStar had already paid to make the plan a reality.

EverStar was going to showcase the Blue Ridge Vista project as a masterpiece of environmental, social, and corporate governance, all topics which had now dominated the news and political landscape ad nauseum. EverStar was planning this event for Blue Ridge Vista and the rest of the country. The Blue Ridge Vista project encapsulated all the essential elements of a socially tempered and environmentally sensitive vision.

The construction project would be net zero for carbon emissions. All the construction equipment would be electric vehicles (funded by a EverStar LLC that was minority-owned, supposedly). The construction company was run by a minority female and was a certified Women's Business Enterprise (100 percent funded by EverStar LLC.) There was also a list of Minority Business Enterprises that would be awarded contracts for the project. The list of construction subcontractors was extensive, all in the EverStar family.

The WBE portion of the contract required an 18 percent participation since federal funds were being used. On a project of this size, the Women's Business Enterprise upcharges were over $35 million alone. On a multibillion-dollar project, it would be relatively easy for EverStar to hide those monies. Even if there was some blowback, which was unexpected, EverStar could rely on the media and their politicians to carry their water, all the time citing the social significance and tremendous financial impact of the project.

This was exactly how EverStar rolled in the financial and equity markets. EverStar knew that every time a project like this was on the horizon, all they had to do was make some calls to their DC connections.

The Knights would face a significant hurdle to knock these guys out. Maybe it was unrealistic to think that there was anything they could do to stop what they sensed was inevitable.

As it was now, the news and print media were on call, along with the DC pols. EverStar had all the wheels moving. There would be only a few weeks before they would formally notify the media of their planned announcement. The EverStar advance team was directed by R. Fitzgerald (Fitz) Walker, who was always quick to share that he was the great-great-grandson of the famous arms manufacturer. His mother had decided to name her son after her grandfather.

Fitz was over six feet tall, in his early forties, and good looking, with gelled short dark hair and piercing blue eyes. He traveled with two henchmen to maintain just the right business distance in case something ever went off the rails in his EverStar world. He had three cell phones: two for business, one for his mistress. Fitz had the blessing of the CEO to operate just this side of the law, and he barely did. He also traveled with a two-person security detail. His arrogance entered a room before he did. This guy had made many corporate messes but somehow managed to escape any trouble. His families' wealth was the only thing that kept him employed, ironically, outside their own empire.

In the late nineties, the family had been advised by their financial and social consultants that diversifying their generational wealth would be in the family's long-term best interests. The consultants sensed that political and social pressures along with global sentiment, would make the core business interests more challenging to protect, especially going into a new century. Their advice was to partner with a PE firm that had an excellent political posture to protect the millions that the family was going to inject into the new enterprise.

Randolph, the grandson of the founder, had a college classmate whom he knew from his Harvard days and had followed his meteoric rise within the EverStar Group. Randolph's attorney made a call to schedule lunch and to discuss a business proposal. The short story is that the family, not the business empire, was going to offer to inject twenty-five million dollars into the EverStar Group. There was one catch: R. Fitzgerald (Fitz) Walker was part of the deal. The family had seen enough of this Fitz and wanted him off their books. He had screwed up everything he had touched, but for $25 million, the EverStar CEO was convinced he could live with the problem. Twenty-five million dollars in the late nineties was enough to transform the EverStar Group into a major power player all over the world. Little would EverStar know how much of a fuckup Fitz was, but they would soon find out.

Today Fitz and his team arrived at Blue Ridge Vista via one of EverStar's corporate jets. Fitz had persuaded the EverStar CEO to have the event on a Wednesday so that the golf pros would have two days off before going to their next tournament. His suggestion made sense, so the PR firm was notified to implement their plan of action to coincide with the EverStar announcement. Fitz had also convinced the CEO that the golf course could be completed in time to get it on the FedEx Cup schedule in two years. EverStar would have to expedite the land deal, but that could happen.

Building a championship course in two years would be a real challenge, but EverStar had all the money needed. Fitz also planned to add some more patio homes to the existing Blue Ridge Vista footprint for all the pros and special guests. The golf tournament would also provide the perfect venue to presell building lots to help cashflow the project. Fitz admired his plan, but he admired himself more because that was the kind of guy he was.

He was going to quarterback the entire project and event via his underlings, as he called them. The guy was a real gem. He had few friends and he deserved it. An avid golfer, Fitz knew many of the pros on a first-name basis, as he was quick to point out to anyone who would listen.

Through all of this, there was one thing that the EverStar CEO was not sharing about their project, including with Fitz, something they learned when they jumped in front of the initial buyer of the land adjacent to Blue Ridge Vista. If revealed, this would entangle and possibly stop the entire deal. This was the main reason that EverStar had added two new board members to help them move more quickly now that they had their plan in motion.

Chapter Nineteen:

Round Table IV

There would be several conversations at dinner at Sal's for the fourth-round table. First would be the update on De-Lo's grandmother: she was resting comfortably, receiving the best possible care, and enjoying her meals and time with him daily. Given Rose's diagnosis and all that De-Lo was dealing with, he was appreciative of how his friends had helped and made it possible for him to be close to his grandmother.

EverStar was another subject, and it required more of their attention and focus. T had made some calls and learned more about how the transaction had gone down. Unbeknownst to him, EverStar had a young attorney they introduced to one of the Kaufman Law partners at a dinner to some of the DC elite crowd. It was suggested that she would make a great addition to their firm because of her background and excellent education—her specialty was real estate.

T recalled that she was bright, liked to work, and would always stay late to complete projects, something he attributed to her age. There was another part of her work outside the firm, however, that he somewhat questioned but never bothered to challenge. She liked politics, a lot. She attended many of the political dinners that T and others in the firm tried to avoid.

The Kaufman Law Firm tried to fly under the radar politically, realizing that a neutral, independent facade was best in the long run for the practice's reputation.

Allana Metcalf turned up the volume needle politically at the Kaufman Law Firm, and her father was a top executive at EverStar. And he spared no expense: Allana attended Yale University as an undergraduate, as well as Yale Law School.

T was getting sick as he learned the story about the new Kaufman attorney. She was the one who had reviewed all the contract documents when he went on his family vacation.

Sal had cleared getting a utility vehicle from Ruiz for their trip back to the orchard. He explained they would ask De-Lo to come along just in case they needed some extra muscle to move some of the larger tree limbs. Ruiz was OK with the vehicle use and including De-Lo on the excursion. The only thing was to ask De-Lo if he would join them tomorrow.

The guys were arriving for dinner. Ben was first, walking by the drawer in the living room and getting the swords for the meeting. Buddy and T came in together. The nap had done them all good.

Sal was putting the finishing touches on the food tray with the usual genoa salami, pepperoni, asiago cheese, marinated olives and roasted red peppers, and a loaf of fresh Italian bread—a match made in heaven. He had two bottles of homemade wine on the table, and Ben had already started pouring some for each of them, filling his glass last. The swords were in their correct positions, and with that, Sal said, "Mangiamo!"

"You know, I love that," said Ben. "Me too," said Buddy.

"Count me in on that," said T. "Thaddeus," T continued.
"What the heck, T?" said Ben. "Who's Thaddeus?"

"Me," said T. "That's what T stands for: Thaddeus."

"Boy," said Ben. "I'm glad we shortened your name to T. Just
kidding. Thaddeus has a cool ring to it."

"In the interest of full disclosure, I wanted you guys to know,
so that's it. Not too exciting, but that is my real first name."

"Thanks for sharing," said Buddy. "Now...Mangiamo," said
Ben. "And beve."

After the round table, T took his time walking home. His mind
had been working overtime. T always enjoyed the gatherings
with Ben, Buddy, and Sal, even though it was not in his DNA
to have a group of friends like the Knights. It made him realize
just how boring it was to hang around with a bunch of attorneys.

T was glad that he had invested his time, energy, and talent
in helping De-Lo so that he could be close to his grandmother
now. The EverStar issue, however, was another challenge to
be dealt with, and T was looking forward to doing battle with
those bastards.

T's final days at his law firm were a blur at best. He had
been on a rare family vacation two weeks prior to being voted
out of the firm by the senior partners. He had been very vocal
in his disapproval of the EverStar $5 million retainer for "any
interference" the Kaufman Law Firm might encounter closing
the acquisition of the 850-acre tract of land and the Blue Ridge
Vista Senior Living Center. Every photo on his wall, every award
he had received for the firm just opened a floodgate of emo-
tions: joy, serenity, pride, anxiety, and anger. He did his best to

manage his composure out of respect for his father and the few friends he had left at the firm.

T had confided in one of his few remaining friends at the firm what he had learned about the new junior attorney and her connection to EverStar, something he hadn't known before. It was painful for him to admit how disappointed he was in learning how EverStar had managed to infect so many parts of corporate America and the politics of Washington, DC.

T's further digging via his few friends still at the firm revealed that EverStar was planning something of a dress rehearsal before their big announcement. An advance team of lower-level EverStar minions would be coming to Blue Ridge Vista to review the logistics and the perfect location for their announcement. This crew wanted to do a thorough site analysis for the senior team at EverStar. The rehearsal would happen in two weeks.

James and Michael decided that Abbey could handle the details of the preparation for the upcoming EverStar rehearsal meeting. They once again concluded their talents would be better spent managing the bigger picture of trying to endear themselves to the EverStar execs who could help with their own career aspirations. They were on an email chain that advised them that

R. Fitzgerald (Fitz) Walker would take the lead on the upcoming EverStar visit. James and Michael had heard some pretty wild stories about the guy called Fitz, and if half of it was true, they wanted to make sure they sucked up to him in the best way possible. Fitz was the EverStar big-picture guy. His minions would handle the minutia.

Abbey was more than qualified to manage the logistics for the planned rehearsal. She had already demonstrated her ability to handle much larger management tasks: preparing quarterly financials, overseeing budget meetings, implementing new analytic reports that compared department performance against industry data, and more. Abbey was no doubt a little rough around the edges, maybe way more, but her skills and competitive personality made her a highly valued executive team member. She had earned the respect of all the department leaders at Blue Ridge Vista for the work she did and her respect for and acknowledgment of their work. She joined in to get things done. She would delegate tasks when appropriate and would praise accomplishments in a group setting. She was what you wanted in a leadership role.

The preparation for the upcoming rehearsal would be a breeze. Abbey would be the executive coordinator to assist in every aspect of the event. She was going to do her best to be an indispensable part of any transition team. She had an excellent knowledge of the Blue Ridge Vista facility, and in fact, she could have easily handled the CEO job. Sal knew that Abbey was already doing James and Michael's jobs. Her attitude and people skills needed some work, but Sal sensed that she was more than willing to try to improve. Time would tell what progress she was making. There was one thing Abbey was not aware of, and that was the EverStar advance team and Fitz. Their meeting would come soon enough.

Sal, Ben, and Buddy listened as T described what he had learned through his contact at his old firm. His pain was evident in the details he shared. The obvious question was how his old firm had been transformed into something he didn't even recognize. What had been a great law practice had provided tremendous lifestyles for so many families. The firm's philanthropic contributions were massive. Each year, the firm's steering committee devoted countless hours to planning major fundraising events for the families and charities of the inner city of Washington, DC. They were good people, and it made T proud because he knew it would have made his father proud. But not now.

The Knights had all the updates on the recent events. There would be more intel to uncover, but for tonight, they had all been briefed.

Sal, Ben, and Buddy just stared at one another, wanting to say something of comfort to T. It was hard to believe that large corporations could manage the minutiae of something so disgusting, but T's law firm and EverStar had taken deceit to a new level with their intentions for Blue Ridge Vista.

T was very calm now and looked at his solemn-faced friends.

"What the hell is wrong with you guys? You look like shit. Cheer up. We're going to get these guys, trust me. Let's eat, OK, Sal?"

All that was left to do was finish the antipasto and have another glass of wine, or vino, as Ben preferred to say.

Tomorrow would be another long day.

Chapter Twenty:

Back to the Orchard

By 9:00 a.m. the next day, everyone was at Sal's ready to go. Ruiz was kind enough to have one of his guys drive Sal and the crew to the orchard. Ruiz didn't want to have an issue by letting someone else use a Blue Ridge Vista vehicle. He even included some goggles and work gloves for the guys. De-Lo was the last to arrive after having breakfast with his grandmother.

"Sorry I'm late," De-Lo said. "Not a big deal," said Ben.

"What it be, B? Nice to see you," said De-Lo.

"What it be B?" Ben looked at De-Lo, not sure of his question. "Na, c'mon now, B, that be you, Ben, OK?"

"Oh, I got it now, I think," said Ben. "Oh, you got it, B; trust me."

"Thank you, De-Lo. So now I'm B."

"Yes, you are, B. B is B, and T is T. What you say to that, Holmes?"

"I say very cool, De-Lo; you're a poet. We appreciate you taking the time to join us. We didn't know if Sal told you that he might put you to work this morning," said Buddy.

De-Lo laughed.

"He forgot to tell me that part of the project," he said, laughing again.

"OK, let's go," said Sal. They all hopped into the off-road vehicle. At their age, getting in and out was the hardest part of this project. They moaned and groaned as they finally sat down.

"Hold on," said Sal, and off they went, slowly, avoiding as many bumps as possible. "So," De-Lo said. "What's with this spot at Blue Ridge Vista that's got you guys going like this? Some hidden treasure?"

"No," said Buddy. "We were just out walking a week ago and stumbled onto it. We didn't have anything with us to get a better look. We thought we would get some tools, rope, and, you know, somebody younger and stronger. It was Sal's idea to put you to work. Hope you don't mind."

De-Lo just smiled and laughed again, looking at Sal. "I told Ruiz we were coming down here to pick up some of the fallen debris so that I could do some woodworking. We need to confide in him about what we really have found."

"But we want to see what's hidden under the fallen trees. That's where you come in," said Sal.

"I have to be honest with you, De-Lo," said T. "We all thought it would be a good idea if you came with us."

"Yes, we did," said Ben and Buddy.

"Well, I'm glad I'm here...I guess," said De-Lo.

They got to the old orchard area at about 9:30 a.m. Looking around now, they had a much better view of the entire area. This time, they all walked around the area where the trees had fallen, trying to get a closer look. The day was clear, and the sun made their inspection easier.

The overgrown brush was blocking most of the view, but they were able to make out what looked like a small, crushed roof and pieces of rough-cut wood.

Ben found a better view as he made his way into the brush.

"Please be careful, Ben," said Sal. "We don't want anyone to get hurt."

T grabbed a hatchet that Ruiz had put in the bed of the utility vehicle. Buddy reached for the heavy-duty pruning shears to cut the trash shrubs as Ben walked closer to the pieces of wood and the old roof.

They were clearly able to see what a small and old structure it was.

Ben called De-Lo and Sal to come around to where they were to look at what they were able to see. With the clearing of the branches and twiggy trees, the sun shone through, and they could see much better.

This is where they needed De-Lo to help them if they were going to find out what was under all the fallen trees and limbs. The place that Ben and T had cleared was the best spot to get a better look. De-Lo moved in closer, using the tools at an energetic pace. He saw an old, broken-down door and more rough-cut wood. His goggles were fogging up a bit from the heat and his exertion. He was getting excited, as though he had found a hidden treasure, talking to all of them as he lifted the old door away from obstructing his view.

"Hey, can you see if Ruiz put a flashlight in the back of the truck?" De-Lo asked. "I'll look," said T, moving at a faster pace as the excitement built for all of them. "Got it," said T. "Here you go," he said as he tossed it to De-Lo. "Be careful."

There was enough clearance for De-Lo to bend down and peek into the opening. The stale and moldy smell was not unexpected.

"Can you see if there is a mask in the truck?" De-Lo asked. Buddy went looking and digging in the back of the truck.

"No mask, but I found some towels. Maybe you can cover your face and mouth with this."

"Great idea," said De-Lo, as he wrapped the towel around his face as best, he could, thinking it would work. His goggles were fogging up more now.

"Be careful," said Buddy again.

The flashlight exposed a dirt floor, the remnants of a fireplace with an old pot lying on its side, and some pieces of what looked like furniture, some still intact. De-Lo was describing each item as he pushed through the inside of what he determined was an old house.

"You guys should see this. I wish I knew how old this stuff is," said De-Lo.

Sal offered to be the next explorer. "You mind if I come in there, De-Lo?" he asked. "No, c'mon in, but don't get any ideas about gettin' fresh with me. I know you old guys don't get much action anymore," De-Lo said.

They all just laughed, and it felt good. De-Lo had just made their day.

"OK, slide over, big guy. Don't you try anything on me; hands to yourself," Sal said. De-Lo just smiled, shaking his head as he slid out to make room for Sal.

"Wow, this is amazing. I mean look at this!" said Sal. "We can't," said Ben, laughing his big laugh. "C'mon, tell us what you see," said T.

Sal pulled out what looked like a piece of an old chair that was underneath a broken table. "I think a family lived here a long time ago," said Sal. He handed the broken chair to De-Lo and kept looking around. He moved closer to where the old fireplace was and noticed a piece of stone on the dirt floor. Sal assumed it was part of an old hearth as he brushed away layers of dirt. He reached for the flashlight De-Lo had handed him when he got inside. He was talking to all of them as he continued exploring.

The hearthstone was massive, at least two inches thick and over twenty inches wide, close to forty inches long. Sal's knowledge of carpentry and construction told him it would have taken at least two people to put the hearthstone in place. Sal continued to brush the dirt from the stone. On the corner of the stone were crude chisel marks; Sal brushed more dirt away and saw the year 1779 roughly etched in the stone. He brushed more dirt away from the entire stone to find another roughly etched marking, this one a name, Adams, almost in the middle. A chill ran up his spine.

It couldn't be, he thought...could it? Sal froze, still bent over in the small space, touching history with his rough and dirty hands. The cold and damp stone felt soothing. He could feel tears welling up but still stared at the space around him like he was in a museum. He didn't want to move. Sweat was beading on his forehead, streaming into his tears. He took in a quiet, deep breath. He was overcome by his mental journey into American history.

He asked the guys to come closer to the small entrance they had created. He didn't want to yell out of respect for the Adams family; he felt like he was a guest in their home.

Sal stuck his head out from the space, dirty, sweaty, and grimy.

"Geez, Sal, you look like shit," said Buddy, never being at a loss for honesty.

"Maybe, but I feel great," said Sal calmly as he continued to crawl out of the entryway and struggled to get to his feet. "I have something for you guys." He reached his dirty, sweaty, and grimy hands out to touch each of them, preparing to share the newly discovered history with his best friends.

"What the heck are you doing, Sal?" De-Lo asked.

"I want you all to meet the Adams family. You were just in their 1779 home, and this is a remembrance."

"What, what do you mean?" asked Ben, staring at the dirt on Sal's face and his own hands. "What's going on?"

"I'm not following," said T. "Help us out."

"I think we have uncovered the home of a famous American family; I can't be sure which Adams family lived here, but one of them did, a very long time ago."

"Well, what do we do?" asked De-Lo.

They all just looked at one another in shock and continued to stare at Sal, who was covered in a dirty mess as he just smiled. How could this be?

De-Lo handed him a part of the old chair that he had found, and Sal looked it over, noticing the workmanship on the seat and arms and the way the chair was joined.

"Guys, we just discovered a museum," said Sal. "I'm no authority on this stuff, but this chair and that hearthstone date this place to the 1770s. Holy shit!"

"You know what," said T. "We just found a way to make those EverStar guys lose everything, and maybe someone at my old firm will go to jail. Our firm did the title search on this parcel before EverStar acquired it out of receivership. The judge was more interested in getting the Medicare fraud issues resolved and accepted the EverStar offer to move the resolution along."

"Please explain," said Ben.

"Wow," said Buddy. "Now it makes sense to me. When we were doing our due diligence on the three pieces of property that make up Blue Ridge Vista, one of the out-of-state sellers had this section of land in their family for well over two hundred years. We were told they would never sell. My buyer offered over three times what it was worth, or at least we thought—about twelve million dollars. It took them a while to decide because there were several great-grandchildren involved. In the end, they took the—"

"Yes, and in the end, they took the EverStar money. Fifteen million dollars, to be exact," said T. "Please excuse me for interrupting you, Buddy. I was having some trouble remembering all the details, as that transaction closed when I was with my family on a rare vacation.

"Our firm had to sign a nondisclosure agreement when the transaction was completed. I never did see all the documents, but in my heart, I am sure this was what the rest of the firm wanted. I did not.

"Next thing I knew, I was being forced to accept a severance package—a generous one, but I didn't want to leave," T said.

"How in the heck could they do that to you, T?" Buddy asked. "It doesn't sound legal to me," said Sal.

"Could you sue them?" asked Ben.

"It was completely legal. They called a special meeting of the senior partners when I was on vacation. They took a vote to revoke my partnership in the firm. It really sucked, I gotta tell you."

"I'm sorry that happened to you, Mr. Kaufman," said De-Lo. "Thanks. Please call me T."

"Now what do we do?" asked Sal, the others listening for advice.

"How does this sound?" said T. "You know that EverStar dress rehearsal that the EverStar JV is planning? Well, I think we should do some surveillance. We show up, and each of us gets in front of one of their people individually. We let them know we are onto their game and have evidence that will cost EverStar everything."

"De-Lo, if you could ask Ruiz permission to attend to help us with our work for the gathering, that would be great," asked T.

"Sounds exciting. If Ruiz gives me the green light, I'm in," said De-Lo. "Great," they all agreed.

There was a lot yet to do. They all jumped in the utility vehicle and headed back to their homes. De-Lo would be joining his grandmother for lunch.

"De-Lo, thank you so much for all your help today. We couldn't have gotten this done without you!" said T.

They all agreed.

The Knights had work to do. Ben was going to do some recon work to gather more info on the attendees. Buddy wanted to review whatever documents were still at his agency. He clearly remembered the section of the property in question and the months it had taken to review the deed and complete the title search. T would work through one of his moles at the Kaufman Law Firm to learn who had given the documents to EverStar and who had signed the nondisclosure agreement.

T remembered that a former EverStar executive had outbid EverStar the first time the Blue Ridge Vista property was on the market. EverStar's patience had really paid off, as they now owned this beautiful Blue Ridge Vista for a mere fraction of the initial price. Blue Ridge Vista was a victim of COVID-19 and financial mismanagement.

Sal needed to share what they had just discovered with Ruiz and pledge him to secrecy.

The Knights' plan for EverStar and the survival of Blue Ridge Vista were at stake.

Chapter Twenty-One:

AMAZING GRACE

De-Lo did his best to clean up for his grandma. He had gotten quite the workout helping the guys down at the orchard. He was glad he could help and enjoyed being a part of the expedition. He was looking forward to sharing his morning adventure with his grandma.

When De-Lo knocked on his grandma's door, he could hear someone talking with her. It was Dr. Colby.

"Excuse me," said De-Lo. "I can come back."

"Absolutely not," said Rose. "Dr. Colby and I were just finishing our talk. Please come on in. You and I have some Bible reading." Then she turned to the doctor.

"Thank you, Dr. Colby," said Rose. "I appreciate your time, more than you know."

"You are most welcome, Rose. I'll be in touch. Take care, De-Lo."

Rose's lunch was on her tray right next to her Bible, which was open to Psalm 23. De-Lo walked around the tray to give her a kiss on her forehead. "Grandma, you haven't touched your food. Let me help you eat, and then we can read the Bible, OK?"

"You know, De-Lo, I'd rather you read to me, if you don't mind. I can eat after we hear God's Word."

"Whatever you want, Grandma." As De-Lo sat down next to her, he could see a gentle smile on her face. She looked so calm, he thought.

"I'm sorry I was late, Grandma. I was helping Sal and the guys on a scavenger hunt."

"Not to worry, De-Lo. I'm just glad you're here. Go ahead and read to me, please."

"Sure thing."

De-Lo reached for the Bible, which was already open and marked with a prayer card. "We haven't read this part of the Bible before, have we, Grandma?"

"I don't believe so. Go ahead."

"The Lord is my shepherd; I shall not want. He maketh me to lie down in green pastures: he leadeth me beside still waters."

Something was wrong. De-Lo knew how much his grandma loved it when he read to her, but this part of the Bible seemed different today. He glanced at Rose, and her eyes were closed. She was resting quietly, and he was glad. She needed her rest. He kept on reading.

"He restoreth my soul: He leadeth me in the paths of righteousness for His name's sake."

De-Lo glanced over again at his grandma and noticed her head had shifted slightly to one side. He got up, touched her hand, and shook it gently.

"Grandma," De-Lo whispered, a little louder. "Grandma... can you hear me?"

Tears were streaming down his face, and he let out a heavy gasp, crying like he had never cried in his life, holding his grandma's hands, kissing her on her forehead.

Dr. Colby had stayed outside by Rose's door as she had asked. She had also asked Dr. Colby to talk with De-Lo and explain that this was the way she wanted to leave this world. Her wish for De-Lo was to continue the progress he was making at Blue Ridge Vista.

Dr. Colby knocked on the door, asking permission to enter. De-Lo, still in tears, opened the door. Dr. Colby placed his hand on De-Lo's shoulder to try to comfort him in some way.

"Your grandmother was a remarkable woman, De-Lo. I know you don't need me to tell you that. We talked regularly during my visits with her about you and the tremendous strides you have made here at Blue Ridge Vista. She was so proud of you."

Still sobbing, De-Lo said, "I don't know what I'm going to do. I mean, how am I going to live without her? It ain't fair."

"Your grandmother mentioned that some older men you have met here at Blue Ridge Vista have taken an interest in your progress," Dr. Colby said. "She thought they would be great to lean on until you are able to leave this place, if that's what you want. She also mentioned Judge Carmichael, who has been following your progress here at Blue Ridge Vista. She thought he would also be able to help you. She mentioned that when you were in court, he seemed to have a genuine interest in what you planned to do with your life. I think these people would be a great support for you, if you ask them," Dr. Colby said. "Do you think you can do that?"

Still sobbing, De-Lo said, "Yes, I can."

"OK," Dr. Colby said. "You can stay with your grandmother as long as you like. I have told the nurses to get you anything you need. You can call me anytime. I will be glad to offer any help that I can, OK?"

"Thank you, Dr. Colby. I appreciate all that you did for my grandmother. My grandma was everything to me."

"I understand, I do," he said.

De-Lo just sat by his grandmother for about fifteen more minutes, trying to get himself together. How was he going to do all of this? A funeral, the cemetery plot? He sobbed more, covering his face with his hands, trying to breathe.

He wiped the tears from his eyes as best he could. As he walked by the nurses' station, he asked what he needed to do for his grandmother now. The nurse told him that Dr. Colby was still handling some of the reports that he needed to complete. De-Lo asked if he could talk with him. The nurse told him she would ask and to wait right where he was.

She returned and said, "Dr. Colby will be right out."

"Thank you very much," De-Lo said as he stared at the ceiling lights.

"De-Lo, what can I help you with?" Dr. Colby asked.

"I was going to talk with some of the guys that my grandma told you about and ask them for some help. Will my grandma be OK while I'm gone?"

"Yes, she will," he replied. "We will have your grandma moved to a different part of this unit until you let us know what your plans are, OK?"

"Yes, that would be a big help until I can get this figured out. Thank you again, Dr. Colby."

De-Lo left the health-care side of the Blue Ridge Vista building and walked down the drive to Sal's home, wondering what he was going to say.

As he walked up Sal's sidewalk, he noticed Sal in the side yard near his tomato plants.

Sal glanced up and paused as he noticed De-Lo's face. "Are you all right, De-Lo?" De-Lo stopped in his tracks, bent his head down, and cried.

"It's my grandma," he said. "She's gone."

Without hesitation, Sal grabbed De-Lo and hugged him while he continued to cry. Sal held on and did his best to try to comfort his friend.

"I'm so sorry, De-Lo. What can I do to help you?"

Trying to work through his tears and still trembling, De-Lo said his grandma was at the health-care section of the facility. De-Lo needed to make funeral arrangements and didn't know how.

"De-Lo, we're your friends," said Sal. "We'll help you. Come on and sit down. Let me get you something to drink. I'm gonna call Ben, T, and Buddy. Please sit down."

Sal asked the guys to come over as soon as they could. He shared that De-Lo needed their help. One by one, they walked into Sal's apartment, noticing De-Lo sitting in the kitchen.

"What's up? What happened?" asked T.

Sal said, "I have some bad news. De-Lo's grandma just passed away." There was a stunned silence. "What?" asked Buddy. "When?"

"Just now," De-Lo said.

"I'm so sorry," said Buddy, placing his hand on De-Lo's shoulder.

Ben was motionless, listening to the others before he could gather himself to offer comfort to De-Lo. He waited, not ashamed of tears, and then hugged De-Lo, not saying anything.

"I just don't know what to do," he answered. "I don't know anything about how to plan a funeral or contact the cemetery or secure any of the arrangements."

"That's where we can help you, if you'll let us," Buddy said.

Trying to stay composed, De-Lo responded, "Please. I need your help."

T put his arms around De-Lo to try to comfort him. "Let's sit down and see what we can do now."

"If it's OK with you, De-Lo, I'm going to call the nurses' station and talk with them so we can figure out how we can help."

"Thank you very much, Mr. Kaufman. I mean T."

Sal took De-Lo's glass to refill it while Buddy and Ben sat down next to him in the living room. He grabbed a bottle of wine and some glasses. Sal asked if De-Lo was thinking of a church service for his grandma and if he could have the name of her church.

"Is there any family you would like us to contact?" asked Ben.

"My grandma's sisters are all gone. I don't know where any of their children are. My grandma had some friends at church from when she sang with the choir, but as far as family goes, you guys are the closest thing I got."

Tears were streaming down their faces as they tried not to make eye contact.

T came back into the living room after speaking with Dr. Colby. "We can help De-Lo with planning the arrangements tonight and call the nurses' station in the morning, OK, De-Lo?"

"I don't know what to say," he said.

"You don't need to say anything," said T. "We'll figure this out together, OK?" They all sat down to help De-Lo get a bit more at ease.

Sal was preparing some food in the kitchen so they could try to talk a little more about a way to comfort De-Lo, if possible. They couldn't imagine being in his position, and they only wondered how De-Lo could shoulder this on his own. Now, he wouldn't have to.

De-Lo shared some stories about when he was younger and how Rose was the only constant in his life. He told the guys a couple of the sayings that were her life lessons. "It's not what you have…it's what you do with what you have," she had told De-Lo at least a hundred times. She also said: "I'm not ever going to make excuses for you, so you'd better never let me hear you making them for yourself,"

"You know what's right—do it," and, "If you want respect, you need to earn it."

That last one was one De-Lo was still trying to figure out.

The guys were astounded. De-Lo's recollection was incredible.

Buddy was trying to think of the right thing to say after hearing De-Lo share his grandmother's wisdom. He knew he was sometimes awkward in these moments but felt an urge to say something.

"Thank you, De-Lo," Buddy said. That was all he could manage to say. It was perfect. "Your grandma was a very smart person, De-Lo," Buddy said.

De-Lo related that his grandma's life was all about survival and doing her best for him.

They talked a bit longer and planned for the morning. Sal was going to call the church and talk with the minister about Rose's passing and ask for his assistance in contacting her friends. T was going to meet with the nurses in the morning and have De-Lo go with him so he would know everything they would be talking about. Buddy and Ben were going to talk with the funeral home director. They had all agreed to cover all the expenses for everything, and they were glad they could help. They all needed a good night's sleep.

They finished the food and made sure De-Lo was comfortable with what they discussed.

He thanked them again and again.

"Why don't we get some sleep?" Ben said. "Great idea," said De-Lo.

"We'll talk in the morning," Buddy replied.

They all walked toward the door of Sal's home, exchanging good nights.

Chapter Twenty-Two:

THE REVIVAL

y morning, Sal had been on the phone with Reverend Moore at Ebenezer Baptist Church. T had made the arrangements for Rose's body to go to the funeral home that Reverend Moore had recommended.

Reverend Moore suggested having a church service on Thursday with the visitation at the church. The choir would perform, and Rose's friends would help make this a special memorial in her honor. The burial would follow.

De-Lo approved of it all, including Reverend Moore's request for De-Lo to offer the eulogy, which made him nervous. De-Lo confided in Reverend Moore that he didn't want to mess up his grandma's funeral service. Reverend Moore put De-Lo completely at ease by assuring him that his grandma would be honored by her grandson's words.

The Knights had prepared to take De-Lo to lunch in town after all the arrangements had been finalized. They wanted to make sure he was OK with the way the plans had been made. He was fine with everything, but he was embarrassed to tell the guys he didn't have any clothes good enough to wear. Not a problem at all, they said; they would go shopping after lunch so he could get the right things. He thanked them again and wondered how he could have handled any of this stuff without their help. He didn't realize how glad they were to help him.

They were able to have a little privacy at lunch and learn more about De-Lo's life and the tremendous obstacles that had always been in front of him and his grandmother. Each of them wondered how in the world someone could survive like De-Lo had and not be mad at the world.

The clothing store was right around the corner from the restaurant. None of them had shopped for clothes in some time, and to say they were fashion challenged would be an understatement. They were greeted when they arrived by a young salesclerk who just stared at them, not De-Lo, as they followed him into the store. The guys didn't know they were being checked out as the salesclerk tried to figure out the possible connection.

Who are these white guys following this young black man into the store? she thought but did not say.

"How can I help you today?" she said as she looked at all of them.

"No, it's not us; you can help him," they said as they all pointed at De-Lo. "Well, how can I help you, sir?"

De-Lo was speechless. No one had ever called him sir.

"I'm looking for some dress clothes. Sport coat, shirt, tie, and slacks for a funeral," he said.

"I'm so sorry," she replied. "Shoes too," said Buddy. "Yes, thank you," De-Lo said.

"Let's try on a jacket to see what size you are," said the young lady. "I'm guessing forty-two long," said Buddy.

"How would you know?" asked Ben. "You'll see," said Buddy. "Just wait."

"You're forty-two long. Just need to take up the sleeves a bit, but yeah, your friend there hit it on the nose."

"We need to get the rest of these clothes with alterations today. Is that possible?" asked T. "Let's check out the slacks. I will call about the alterations, but I don't see a problem," she responded.

De-Lo chose pants and picked out two shirts, two ties, a belt, socks, and shoes. He was set. The clothes would be ready in an hour. T slid the young lady a fifty-dollar bill just to make sure.

They went back to the restaurant and sat out on the patio and had some beverages as they waited. There was still more time to talk. De-Lo asked them about what he should say for his grandma's eulogy. He had no idea.

"Share how your grandma helped you through your life. Maybe share a story about growing up," T said.

Sal offered that he could talk about something he had learned from his grandma, like the stories he had shared with them the night before. That would be perfect.

Ben and Sal stayed outside to give De-Lo some breathing space while he picked up the altered clothes. The salesclerk saw them walking toward the store and had already placed his purchase by the dressing room.

"Here you go," she said.

T suggested that De-Lo try everything on, just in case. In about five minutes, De-Lo came out of the dressing room, looking like a million dollars. He had a smile on his face.

"Thank you, guys. I mean, I never had clothes like this in my life."

"Well, it's about time you did," said Buddy. "You look great."

De-Lo felt great. It had been a long time since he could remember feeling like this. "What do you think?" he asked.

"Wow," said T. "I think you do those clothes well."

"I can never repay you guys," De-Lo said.

The salesclerk was still not sure what was going on but smiled gently. "They look good on you," she said.

"We have to get going," said T. "Are you good with this stuff, De-Lo?"

"You bet," he replied.

T settled with the salesclerk, and they were on their way back to Blue Ridge Vista. Tomorrow was going to be a long day.

On the way home, Sal suggested they meet at his home at about 8:00 a.m. The memorial service for Rose would be at 10:00 the next morning. That way they would have time to check in with Reverend Moore in case there was anything they could do to help. As they arrived at Blue Ridge Vista, Ben told everyone to get a good night's sleep.

There were no arguments.

They arrived at Sal's before eight o'clock, each letting himself in. They suited up nicely; De-Lo would not recognize them. De-Lo was the last to arrive, and the wait was worth it. He looked like something out of *GQ* magazine. They smiled and asked who he was. De-Lo smiled and thanked them again.

"We need to get going," Sal said.

They arrived at the church and were greeted by Reverend Moore. The funeral home had placed Rose's casket in front of the altar. Reverend Moore walked over to De-Lo. "Let's go see your grandmother Rose," he said.

Reverend Moore gently placed his hand on De-Lo's shoulder, and they walked closer to De-Lo's grandma. He stared down, tilting his head slightly while trying to hold back tears.

"It's OK, De-Lo," said Reverend Moore. "It's OK."

De-Lo breathed a little easier, thinking how peaceful his grandma looked. "Would you give me a moment with my grandma?" De-Lo asked.

Reverend Moore nodded and backed off quietly. De-Lo reached down to hold his grandma's hands, kissed her on her forehead, and said, "Thank you, Grandma, for all your caring, and I love you."

The Knights were trying to avoid making eye contact with De-Lo so he wouldn't see them crying. After his moment with his grandma, De-Lo asked them to join him beside her casket. As if they were having a private service, De-Lo said, "Grandma, these are the guys I was talking to you about. I told them they were my new family. I think I scared them."

Tears streamed down their faces as De-Lo smiled in gratitude for his new old friends.

Reverend Moore walked over and whispered to De-Lo that more people were starting to enter the church. They should move to the side and greet their guests.

Sal, Ben, T, and Buddy thought it best if they moved to an area about fifteen feet from where the folks had started to assemble in line. It's not a stretch to say that the four of them looked a bit out of place in the church. De-Lo had asked them to be honorary pallbearers for his grandma, and they had accepted. The funeral director showed them where he wanted them to sit for the church service, which was right next to where De-Lo would be sitting. They followed his instructions.

The visitation lasted about two hours, and each of the choir members patiently waited in line to share a story about Rose and express their sympathy. De-Lo remembered many of them, although not their names as much as their faces.

Realizing the same, each of them told him their name and that they remembered De-Lo at Sunday-morning service, that Rose would walk into the back of the church to get her choir robe, and De-Lo would be seated in the second row so she could see him. His mind was wandering back to those days right now.

Reverend Moore whispered in De-Lo's ear, "Are you ready to celebrate your grandma's life?"

With tears in his eyes, he said, "Yes I am, thank you."

They all stood for the first hymn, "Amazing Grace," as De-Lo stared at the stained-glass windows on the front of the church. He had never viewed them from this vantage point before. The middle window depicted Jesus as a child in the temple with the elders. To the right was the nativity, and to the left, Jesus at the crucifixion, his entire life encapsulated in one beautiful piece of art. The morning sun provided a majestic reflection in the church while De-Lo continued his stare as if in a trance.

Reverend Moore walked to the lectern to welcome everyone to the celebration of Rose's life, a life lived for others. The softness of his voice settled De-Lo's nerves. The first reading was from 1 Corinthians 13, which begins, "If I speak in the tongues of men or of angels, but do not have love, I am only a sounding gong or a clanging cymbal."

De-Lo recalled this Bible passage, though he could not remember all the verses except for "but the greatest of these is love."

That was his grandma. Love. His eyes welled up again.

Reverend Moore read a few prepared words and then turned to the choir and back to the congregation. They sang another hymn, "How Great Thou Art." The choir gently swayed in peaceful unison as De-Lo stared intently at the stained-glass windows.

Following the hymn, Reverend Moore introduced De-Lo to those gathered in the church. He provided a brief history of De-Lo's journey and how Rose had provided and cared for him. He turned to De-Lo, extending his hand as he approached the pulpit. De-Lo walked up slowly while he looked at Sal, Ben, T, and Buddy. He smiled and reached into his jacket pocket for what he had prepared.

"Thank you, Reverend Moore, and thank you all so much for honoring my grandma with your presence today. I appreciate the love I feel, and I know my grandma would also.

"I was a problem child for my grandma. I didn't want to be, but I just kept doing stupid things, I must be honest. I wish I had been more responsible when I was younger, but I wasn't. My grandma never gave up on me—never. I thank God these days for her love and caring.

"You know, when you're a kid, you can't think past your next meal or how to stay out of trouble. I got in a lot of trouble.

"I would like to share a story with you about how my grandma would get me to think about the things I did. She did her best to get me to understand how the things I did caused big problems for other people."

De-Lo took a deep breath, his eyes drifting upward at the beauty of the stained glass to calm him.

"I think I was about fourteen, and my choice of friends was not the best. One day, we were just hanging out near the corner. The guys were talking about running into the store and getting something to eat, or at least I thought. One guy was talking loudly and making a real mess.

"The owner came out from behind the counter to see what was going on. It was then that another guy ran behind the counter and beat on the cash register. The owner—Mr. Dias, as I would learn—ran back to stop him from stealing the cash. Mr. Dias's wife, who was in the store, tried to help but was knocked over and hit her head on the display.

"The guys and I ran out of the store. I was afraid, not knowing what the heck had just gone down. The guys, who I thought were my friends, made fun of me because I was scared. I felt sick. I told my grandma what happened, embarrassed that I was involved. She asked me for all the details. I told her everything, crying the entire time.

"She told me to get her purse and take her to the store. Now I was more scared and told her so. She said, 'You should be scared, because you did something stupid and bad.' I felt sick to my stomach, not wanting to go with her, but I had no choice. She grabbed me by the collar of my shirt and pulled me into the store, which was a mess because of the guys who I thought were my friends.

"She said, 'My name is Rose, and this is my grandson, Demetrius Lorenzo Wilson.' Now I knew I was in trouble. She said, 'I understand that some boys came into your store today and stole from you. I apologize. I don't have much, but I will give you what I have, and he will work for free for as long as it takes to pay you the rest. I understand your wife was knocked over, and I hope she is all right.'

"I stood in silence thinking, 'I didn't steal anything; why do I have to work for free?

That's not right.' Boy was I wrong.

"Mr. Dias walked over to my grandma and reached his hand out to thank her for her honesty. There was about two hundred dollars in the register at the time, he explained. I remember my grandma had about fifty dollars and change in her purse, which she handed to Mr. Dias, along with another apology. She paused and pointed at me and said, 'He's good for the rest—and before you say another word, you apologize to Mr. Dias and his wife.'

"You know when you've done something wrong—we all do. But at that moment, I was so scared and proud. Scared for what I did, and proud of my grandma, who did her best to make it right. She didn't have much money—we never did—but she had pride and showed me what courage is.

"On the way home, I remember telling my grandma that I didn't steal anything, that it was the other guys. We walked farther, and she turned and looked me straight in the face. She said, 'You let yourself be part of what they did, and that is just the same. You need to remember that the next time you get a stupid idea like that. Got it?'

"Thoroughly disgusted with myself, I had no response. There was nothing to say. My grandma was about five feet in front of me walking at a pretty good speed. I couldn't defend myself from my own stupidity, and I knew it. Now I felt worse. How could I make it up to my grandma? That's what hurt the most. I tried to catch up to her.

"We kept walking; I kept listening. 'People judge you by what you do. You need to remember that, Demetrius. You gotta promise me. I don't want to have to go through this again with you. Can you promise me and mean it?'

"You know, sometimes you have problems remembering things that happened a long time ago. Well, the walk home with my grandma is as vivid today as it was some five years ago. I would do my best to keep my promise to my grandma. I wish I could tell you I never screwed up again, but I can't.

"I do try to honor my grandma with better decisions that I make. What she taught me still comes into my head more these days, and that's a good thing. I wish she was here so I could tell her so. What I can tell you all is my life is better because of my grandma. And I love her for that.

Thank you all, and thank you, Reverend Moore, and my new old friends from Blue Ridge Vista, my new home."

De-Lo made his way back to the chair beside Reverend Moore for the closing tribute song, "Battle Hymn of the Republic," as the entire church rose.

Rose's casket was turned and positioned for the procession to follow, with Reverend Moore and De-Lo side by side. The official pallbearers, followed by Ben, Sal, T, and Buddy, made their way to the back of the church and waited for Rose's casket to be placed in the hearse.

A brief graveside service was conducted. De-Lo placed a rose on his grandma's casket and cried some more. Buddy, T, Ben, and Sal moved to be closer to De-Lo. As he turned to look into their faces, they all cried. De-Lo did his best to comfort each of them, telling them that everything was going to be OK. After about ten minutes they went back to the church, where the choir had planned for a carry-in lunch.

Reverend Moore had a few words to share and confirmed that De-Lo had indeed done some stupid things during his life, which made De-Lo smile.

"A life lived with a purpose" was how Reverend Moore described Rose. "It's not what you have; it's what you do with what you have." And Rose had done a lot.

With the service completed, many came by to greet De-Lo and extend their sympathy.

The Knights did their best to keep to the side so De-Lo could have some privacy with each of the people who came through the line. The food was almost ready for serving, and the aroma was amazing.

Ben leaned over to Sal. "When do you think we get to eat? I'm hungry," said Ben.

He was overheard by one of the women who was preparing the food. She tapped him on the shoulder and said, "Any time now."

Ben was embarrassed and shook his head as if to say, "Excuse me." She laughed. "I think you're going to like the food," she said.

Ben, never missing a beat, said, "I know I will."

He did his best to wait patiently with the rest of them, and when the line was shorter, they slid in. Sal would try everything, as would all of them, but they each had their favorites and made a return trip. They asked Reverend Moore if they could donate for the food even though they had already given some money for the choir and the church. Reverend Moore said their donation would be gladly accepted.

Following the meal, Ben, Sal, T, and Buddy stayed to help clean up and relax a bit while watching De-Lo in conversation with many of the church members. He seemed calmer. De-Lo and Reverend Moore talked a while longer.

After the church dining area was cleaned, they all spoke with Reverend Moore to thank him again for his help and for providing a shoulder for De-Lo to lean on over these past few days. As they were leaving, Reverend Moore made sure to invite them all back to service and fellowship whenever it would work for them.

Sal thought the drive back to Blue Ridge Vista would be awkwardly silent, but he was wrong. They all had questions for De-Lo about how long his grandma had been a member of Ebenezer Baptist, how many years she sang in the choir, and how long Reverend Moore had been the pastor.

De-Lo was surprised by their interest, which was something he had been getting used to.

He just smiled. They asked De-Lo to let them know if he needed any help with his grandma's things or moving her furniture out of the apartment. The Knights would not be able to do the actual moving but offered to plan for a service to help with the physical labor. Except for some photos and some other personal items, De-Lo had thought about selling everything and giving all the money to Ebenezer Baptist Church. He asked the guys what they thought about his idea.

One more time, they realized how much De-Lo had a heart like Rose's. "Great idea," they all said.

De-Lo was going to call Reverend Moore to ask for his help in coordinating his plan. The Knights knew he would approve.

When they arrived at Blue Ridge Vista, it was nearly six o'clock in the evening. "This old guy is going to relax and get a good night's sleep," Ben said. "Hey Ben, it's only six p.m. What the heck?" De-Lo said.

Ben replied, "This old dog needs his rest; tomorrow we have more work. And besides, I value my beauty rest." He laughed his loud laugh.

"Hey, Ben, we're not far behind you," said T. Sal and Buddy nodded in agreement. "What do you say we meet at my place around ten a.m. and talk about the work we still must do? I'd like to ride down to the orchard one more time," said T. "I have an idea."

"Hope you can join us, De-Lo," said T. "We're going to need your cell phone."

"Whoa, this sounds serious," said De-Lo. "I'll be there."

Chapter Twenty-Three:

THE HOLE CARD

They all slept well that evening. Sal was able to get the utility vehicle again from Ruiz and promised to have it back in less than two hours. Ruiz appreciated that Sal had confided in him about the Knights' discovery. Ruiz promised all of them that his lips were sealed.

They all gathered at T's, sharing how well they had slept and that they looked forward to T's plan with De-Lo's cell phone.

De-Lo was the last one to arrive. He had also slept well, as he told each of them. "You needed a good night's rest the most," Buddy said.

They were ready to get in the utility truck when Buddy said, "I need to tell you all something."

They paused and turned toward him, not knowing what to expect.

"I wanted to tell you this before, when T shared about his departure from his law firm, but I was embarrassed."

"What is it?" asked Ben. The others were staring at Buddy.

"My wife left me. She had an affair with a guy I hired, and she cleaned me out financially. That's why I'm still selling patio homes for Blue Ridge Vista at seventy-five years old. Pretty embarrassing, don't you think?"

"Hell no," said Ben. "Not in the least."

"Are you kidding me?" said Sal. "I'm sorry for what happened to you, but none of us would ever judge you for what happened and for how you deal with it. I admire you. We all do."

De-Lo didn't know what he had gotten himself into with these guys, but he'd just witnessed a painful and personal confession about Buddy's life. He felt uncomfortable, not that it made any difference to him or the way he felt about the Knights.

"You know, I remember when T told us about how he departed his law firm. I wanted you guys to know my story. Not a real happy ending—that is, until I met you old farts. We have more in common than I thought," said Buddy.

"Well, I just couldn't go another day without telling you. I hope you don't mind. Let's get to the orchard," Buddy said. He felt much better now.

"De-Lo, do you have your cell phone?" asked T. "Sure do, and it's fully charged."

"Great," said T. "Let's go."

During the ride to the orchard, Sal thought how hard it must have been for Buddy to share his story with the guys and De-Lo. He was right. It was a real relief for Buddy to get that off his mind.

They arrived at the old orchard, and T asked De-Lo to start recording a video on his cell phone of all of them exploring the ruins in the orchard. T began to narrate as De-Lo panned over the fallen trees and the passageway that they had made to the old farmhouse.

T talked about a Virginia law from the 1800s that was passed to protect homesteads as part of an Original Colony Act, which was still in effect. The Virginia Legislature had updated the act frequently to prevent developers from destroying these historic sites. Sal looked at T and thought about what a smart man he was. They walked closer to the opening, and De-Lo continued to film. T kept the narration focused on what they had discovered about this part of the Blue Ridge Vista property and how Virginia law would protect it from commercial development. The guys were wondering what he planned to do with the video.

Sal offered to go into the house since he was smaller, and Ben was going to help cut back some of the debris that was still hanging from the trees. De-Lo got closer; T continued.

"Our video is going to provide you with what we believe to be proof that this is John Adams's family homestead. We are going to share that evidence with you all," T said.

Sal got closer to the main room, where the large pot was still on its side, right next to the large hearthstone. De-Lo handed him his cell phone and instructed him to not move it too quickly.

"Just take your time and try to get as much of the room as possible, and then focus on the numbers and name chiseled in the stone, OK?" De-Lo said.

Sal followed his instructions completely, wanting to make sure that T would be pleased with what he filmed.

Sal called to Ben, "Tell De-Lo I think I got all of it. I'm going to hand his phone to you; ask him what he thinks."

Ben bent down to get De-Lo's phone and handed it to him.

T and De-Lo pushed Play. The lighting was good, and Sal had done a good job of holding it steady. The focus was great, and the hearthstone with the Adams name and the year were perfect. T's narration to coincide with the video was perfect; it would have the dramatic effect they had hoped.

T said, "This is great. I think we got all that we need here."
He asked De-Lo if he would be able to connect his cell phone
to a monitor. De-Lo thought he could figure it out.

"This was great teamwork, guys. I think we have enough
here to put a big knot in their underwear and make it feel tight,
if you know what I mean," said T.

"Why don't we get together tonight at my place?" offered Sal.
"I sure would like to see the video and explain how you're going
to pull this off, T. Does that sound OK to you guys?"

Before anyone could answer, Ben asked, "What time?"

"The usual," said Sal. "I'll have the food ready. Come whenever it works for you."

"I'll be there a little early to help you, if you don't mind,"
said Ben.

"Perfect," said Sal. "You can test the food to make sure it
tastes OK." Ben just let out one of his large laughs, and Sal
loved it.

"We'd like you to join us, De-Lo, if you want," said Buddy.

"Hell yeah," he replied. "I want to see what's going on. I don't
quite understand what you all are up to."

"Don't worry, De-Lo, after tonight you will. And Buddy,
I think you're going to have grounds for a huge lawsuit made
possible by some of the bad actors at my old firm," said T.

T was convinced that EverStar knew that the last parcel
of property was protected by the old Virginia Homestead Law
and there was no way, once the transaction was made public,
that they could get their huge deal done. He also figured out
that was the reason for the nondisclosure agreement his firm
had to sign that required the closing documents to be sealed.
After all, EverStar had too many favors to repay to politicians,
contractors, and automotive parts entities, all in the EverStar
family of corruption. This deal would cover all their "expenses."

He just had to work through the details and talk about it with the Knights and De-Lo.

"I don't understand," said Buddy. "But I'll be glad to hear the whole thing tonight."

Sal walked toward the utility vehicle and said he needed to return it to Ruiz. They all hopped in for the ride back.

Chapter Twenty-Four:

ROUND TABLE V

At six o'clock, the guys started to roll in. Ben got the swords out of the drawer in the living room and placed them in front of each of the chairs. Sal got another chair for De-Lo; there was plenty of room. Smokey Robinson was providing the music this evening. The antipasto was well prepared, and the aroma was more special tonight considering the work they had done. De-Lo was the last to arrive.

De-Lo didn't know what to make of what was going on other than they all seemed to move about easily, like they all lived at Sal's. He looked around, noticing all of Sal's family photos. He was glad he showed up. The music was perfect.

"Nice crib you got here, Sal. Whoa, who's this beautiful woman in this picture?" De-Lo asked.

"That's my wife, Regina," said Sal. "Isn't she beautiful?"

"Well, hell yes," said De-Lo. "I didn't know you were married to a black woman."

"I was. She died from cancer. I miss her every day. She was my whole life. She was as kind and considerate as she was beautiful."

"I never knew, Sal. I'm sorry."

"Don't be sorry, De-Lo. We had a wonderful life together. Now let's find out what those guys are doing."

"Hey, we're in the kitchen, De-Lo," Buddy said.

"If you want any food, you'd better get in here," said Ben.

"On my way. Wow, what a feast," De-Lo said. "Excellent choice of music, Sal."

"Why, thank you, De-Lo."

"Mangiamo," said Ben.

"What?" said De-Lo.

"That's Italian for 'eat'!" said Ben.

De-Lo noticed the swords on the round table. "Those look lit," said De-Lo.

"What's 'lit'?" asked Sal.

"Cool, cool," said De-Lo. "Where'd you buy those?"

"Sal made them," said Buddy.

"No, Ben made them," said Sal. "No, I didn't," said Ben.

"Yes, you did the hard part," said Sal. "What you did made them special." De-Lo picked one up and studied it while the others talked and ate. "What do you do with them? What are they for?" he asked.

Sal looked at Ben and asked him if he wanted to explain it to De-Lo. "Sure," Ben said.

He told him the story of the wooden swords and what they meant to them and how they symbolized their friendship at Blue Ridge Vista.

"Man, that is way cool," said De-Lo. "You guys are pretty neat, for old guys," he said as he chuckled. "Just messin' with you."

"You'd better get some food," said T. "I know you'll like it." Sal asked if anyone wanted a glass of vino; everyone did.

De-Lo asked, "What's vino?"

"Vino is wine in Italian," said Ben as he walked toward him, looking directly into his eyes, and asked, "How old are you, De-Lo?"

"I'm twenty," he answered.

"Well, I guess you're just going to have to wait," said Ben. "Wait for what?" he replied.

"Wait till you're old enough," said Ben.

De-Lo looked at Ben, astonished, like he couldn't believe what he just said. "Don't worry, guys. I'm legal in Virginia."

"You are? How do you know?" they asked.

"I'm underage and accompanied by a guardian. That'd be you old guys, my new friends.

I'm good. Right, T?" De-Lo asked.

They all smiled. Ben laughed his normal laugh, which was perfect. "You are correct, De-Lo. Virginia code 4.1–305 grants him that right."

"Wow!" said Ben. "OK, Beve."

"Excuse me," said Sal. "Before we do that, I would like to propose a toast to De-Lo's grandmother, Rose.

"We all have learned more about you and your wonderful grandmother. Her love for you is inspirational. May you find your way and know that we are here for you, if you need us."

Raising his glass, Sal said, "To Rose and her grandson, our new, young friend, De-Lo. Salud."

De-Lo gave each of them a hug, tears in his eyes. "You old guys are lit," he said. "Now, go ahead, have a glass of vino, wine."

De-Lo looked at Sal and Buddy, "You guys OK with that?"

"What the hell?" said Buddy. "Beve! Drink!"

Ben gently touched De-Lo on the shoulder and said, "Now this is the good part."

As De-Lo lifted his glass of wine, Ben pointed to the cutting board full of the knowledge of an Italian chef.

"That's prosciutto, dry sausage, genoa salami, marinated garlic olives—my favorite—asiago, provolone, Havarti, and fontina cheese, roasted red peppers, and fresh Italian bread. Mangiamo!" Ben said.

Sal just smiled and gave Ben a huge hug and a kiss on both cheeks, raised his glass, and said, "Salud."

Ben guided De-Lo through the different choices, encouraging him to try some of it all.

Ben was just a natural at making people feel comfortable, thought Sal.

T had taken the time to make some notes following their trip to the orchard. He asked De-Lo if he had brought his cell phone so that they all could see the video. De-Lo suggested making a copy just in case something happened to his phone. T thought it was a great idea, but they would need some help to figure out how to do it. T asked De-Lo to start the video so that the Knights could see and hear what T wanted the media and pols to know if EverStar decided to go forward with their plan for Blue Ridge Vista.

They all watched and listened to the video, clearly making out the structure and most importantly, the hearthstone. T's narration captured what was important, and he provided just the right amount of commentary.

The backdrop of the plan was the first buyer's unknowing attempt to purchase the Blue Ridge Vista property, a historic Virginia landmark. The plan was thwarted by EverStar's aggressive and corrupt interference in the process by a surrogate, as T later learned. A former EverStar executive had cut in front of the initial purchase. T discovered this from his inside contact at his old firm. EverStar had planted their executive in another firm, giving the appearance of a bitter competitive battle for

Blue Ridge Vista. EverStar's intention was to drive the price so high that the other group would not be able to acquire the property. EverStar bowed out when the price was too rich for them. COVID-19 proved to be the equalizer, and EverStar had what they wanted for a fraction of the original price.

T's admission of his old firm's interference in the process and the use of Buddy's work product illegally was the basis for the proposed action that T was willing to take and pay for. T was not about to share that the new, young attorney in their firm, whose father worked for EverStar, was instrumental in the plot. He would share that at the appropriate time.

For now, they would eat and drink and talk as De-Lo studied each of the swords, asking more questions.

"Why are there different-colored stones?" he asked.

Buddy explained that they were birthstones, that everyone had a birthstone. "What month were you born?"

De-Lo answered, "I was born in May."

"Your birthstone is an emerald. A beautiful stone, if I do say so myself. It was my wife's stone too. I made her a ring for our wedding with some small diamonds around it. She loved it."

There was a brief silence. It was the first time Ben had ever mentioned his wife. He smiled. "I miss her. I'm glad I met you guys."

Sal suddenly had an idea that he was going to discuss with Ben after the meeting. T continued with his plan.

"If I'm right, this a huge deal for EverStar, easily north of eight hundred million dollars." He paused as the guys looked at him in disbelief.

"How?" asked Sal.

"Between the land purchase, all of the EverStar-owned companies, the corporate sponsorships, I could be way under on my estimate," he said.

Sal was amazed at how T was able to present all the information concisely and without emotion. That was until T spoke again.

"That's why those bastards are going to pay, pay for what they did to me and Buddy and what they plan to do to us. We're not going to let them. I'm going to enjoy looking those guys right in the eye and watching to see who talks first after we tell them what we found," he said.

"What do you mean, 'We tell them'?" asked Ben. "Don't you mean *you'll* tell them?"

"Whatever," said T. "It's going to be fun when we drop this big bag of shit on them at their press conference, in front of everyone, don't you think?"

"You guys are playing hardball," said De-Lo. "When's the press conference?"

T explained that the date was not yet confirmed but that it would be in about four to five weeks. There was still a lot of work for them to do.

Buddy shared that the Knights met each Monday night at Sal's to recap the work they had done the week before and to plan what they would do the next week.

"Sounds like you guys are on a mission," said De-Lo.

"We sure as hell are," said Ben. "Those EverStar assholes screwed up T's and Buddy's lives, and now we have a plan to pay them back."

"Exactly," said Sal. "T has been amazing, figuring this whole thing out."

T interrupted Sal. "It was you and Ben who noticed what was happening at Blue Ridge Vista.

That started the whole ball rolling."

"What do we do this week?" asked Buddy.

"I'd like to help if you'll let me," said De-Lo.

They all looked at him. Ben said, "We're counting on your help."

"You bet," said T. "The video and getting it hooked up to a monitor are our hole card. We need you."

Before the meeting ended, they reviewed what they were going to be doing the upcoming week. They were all on the same page.

Chapter Twenty-Five:

℞ECON ℬEGINS

℞e-Lo had been working in the Office of Property Management at Blue Ridge Vista for the past three weeks completing reports in the format that his boss, Erica, had designed. He had demonstrated a real interest in learning and assumed other related tasks to help Erica. She had taken time to explain to De-Lo what the reports were and why they were important to her team and the executive management of Blue Ridge Vista.

This week, he would begin to ask and learn more about the audio and visual capabilities of Blue Ridge Vista. He was going to casually inquire about how she used PowerPoint presentations for the executive team. Since De-Lo now had internet access, he would learn more about transferring his video to a presentation format.

While De-Lo was focused on the E Team corridor, Ben was going to survey the ballroom setup for the rehearsal of the EverStar conference. Sal had talked to Ben about De-Lo following the meeting. They were going to make him a sword, just like the ones they had. T and Buddy agreed it would be a great idea. That would be Sal's task for the next few days.

Buddy was going to review the Blue Ridge Vista transaction file to learn more about the deed and title to the southeast portion of the parcel in question. Maybe there was something he had missed when his team was reviewing the documents.

T planned to talk to his contact at the firm and share what they had uncovered.

Monday went by in a blur. They all made real progress. Tuesday would prove to be more eventful for everyone, especially Ben.

They all met for coffee on Tuesday morning at Sal's, stressing to be cautious and not too aggressive in their information gathering. De-Lo and Ben had the more sensitive tasks, and they both knew it and relished their detective abilities. De-Lo said he was getting assignments with more responsibility. He was planning to work through his lunch to get some time for online technical support. He would be able to plug his phone into a monitor and run it through an HDMI cable.

Ben and De-Lo were walking up the main drive to Blue Ridge Vista, talking about what they wanted to get done today. De-Lo walked down the hall toward the E Corridor, and Ben nonchalantly walked around the grand concourse, the ballroom off to his left. He grabbed another cup of coffee, sat down to read the local paper, and studied the large room.

He waited a few minutes, got up, and walked over to the entrance of the ballroom. He decided to walk in, and at the same moment he felt someone at his back. He turned and almost spilled his coffee on a woman.

"Oh, please excuse me," Ben said. "I'm glad I didn't spill my coffee on you."

"Trust me, I'm gladder than you," she replied.

Ben, staring at her name tag, felt a sudden smile on his face. "Something amusing?" she asked.

"Why, no, not at all," Ben, still smiling, answered. "Please, please, I'm curious," she insisted.

"Why, Abbey," he said as he stared at her name tag. "It's nice to meet you."

"Have we met before?" she asked.

"Nope," Ben said.

"You must tell me what is getting you to smile like this after nearly dumping your coffee on me."

Ben was beginning to see what Sal was talking about. He decided to play along briefly. "I've heard some things about you from my friend," he said.

"I hope they were good things," she pushed.

Ben tilted his head a bit. "Absolutely, they were."

"I'm flattered. Would you mind sharing the source of your smile?"

"Uh, well, it was, my good friend, Sal Romano."

"Oh, so Sal's your friend, is he?"

"Absolutely," replied Ben. "He's one of the truly good guys."

"I must admit, Ben, my first meeting with Sal was a bit rocky, but Sal was more of a gentleman than I was a woman. I apologized to him for my behavior—very unprofessional."

"Sal shared with me the rocky start and explained how much of the responsibility you have shouldered. He also said you were a real looker; I mean *are* a real looker. Hope you don't mind; just being honest with you."

"I appreciate that, Ben; thank you kindly." Abbey was trying not to blush.

"You're welcome. We were all talking about the same things we noticed at Blue Ridge Vista since we got here months ago. We were wondering if this place is going to survive. It's the not knowing that is causing us the concern."

"I can absolutely appreciate that. As I explained to Sal, with the new ownership change and reorganization, things are moving quickly. I told Sal I will keep your crew up to speed."

"Well, that's all we can ask for. It's just pissing us off, know what I mean?"

"Completely," Abbey replied. "I'm going to keep digging to get a better read on the EverStar Group. I'm convinced they have bigger plans for Blue Ridge Vista that I don't know about. I'm also sure that James and Michael have been kept out of the loop as well. Those two are as worthless as tits on a boar, know what I mean? You'll have to excuse me; I was raised on a farm in Oklahoma, and sometimes I forget who I'm talking to. I heard that expression when I was a child, and it seems a perfect description of those two jerks. There's no escaping that."

"I'm from Indiana, and that makes perfect sense to me," Ben said, enjoying the lighter conversation and Abbey's casual temperament.

"Let me tell you what I mean about those two knotheads that I didn't share with Sal.

Before I started working here, Blue Ridge Vista's finances were in disarray. In my previous job, I created a report that focused on critical data with footnotes to explain variances in bottom-line results. I reworked the report to fit Blue Ridge Vista's key performance data and presented it to James and Michael as a quarterly summary. The only thing those two assholes commented on was the color of the report and the neat three-dimensional use of the graphs and charts. You can't make that shit up; I mean they were clueless as to the overall content. You'll have to excuse me, Ben, but that's what I deal with daily with those two nimrods."

One more time Ben couldn't resist his patented laugh and excused himself. He could feel Abbey's frustration and wished he could help her. Ben continued to listen to Abbey describe more details about Blue Ridge's lack of management.

"Abbey, you're amazing, Sal was right. I have really enjoyed meeting you. Sorry about almost spilling my coffee on you. Look forward to seeing you again. Have a nice day."

"Thanks, you too—tell me something, Ben."

"Sure, what do you want to know?"

"How did you, Sal, Buddy, and T get to be such good friends in such a short time here at Blue Ridge?"

"It was Sal. He just introduced himself to us, invited us to his house to talk, eat, and enjoy some homemade wine. Really, it was just kinda hanging out. You know, nothing fancy, but pretty cool for old guys. T and Buddy, though, have a deeper connection to Blue Ridge Vista than Sal and I do. Their connection goes back about six years ago to the original purchase of the Senior Living Center and the property, some big—really big—money and questionable stuff that happened. T and Buddy could explain that part to you much better. You should ask them; I'm sure they'd be glad to tell you."

"Maybe I will," said Abbey. "Thanks for sharing."

Ben got another cup of coffee and the newspaper and decided to sit on the veranda and enjoy the morning, the view, and the fresh spring fragrance of the viburnum. It was a beautiful day. Abbey was everything that Sal had described. A bit rough around the edges, which he didn't mind, and very easy on the eyes. She would make a much better ally than enemy; the Knights would have to draw her into their circle of friendship. The best way to do that would be to share with her what they knew about the orchard and what they suspected about the operating funds and financial mismanagement. She would be able to confirm their suspicions about Blue Ridge's inner workings and let them know the date of the EverStar rehearsal.

Abbey Connors had three brothers; two were older. Her father and mother farmed one thousand acres of corn and beans in central Oklahoma. The entire family knew hard work. Her brothers loved her dearly but never made things easy for her, and she wouldn't have had it any other way. Abbey's mother died when Abbey was fourteen, a time in her life when she really needed a mother's love and understanding. Her brothers did their best to try to make her life as normal as they could. One day during school recess, a boy told his friends that he was going to kiss Abbey when she was on the playground. A friend of Abbey's shared the news with her, and when the boy approached her, she busted him in the nose and dropped him to the ground. As she stood over him, she said, "Don't you ever try that again, or I'll kick your ass in front of all your friends. Got it?"

Next thing Abbey knew, she was in the principal's office asking for her older brother to come pick her up and take her home for a three-day suspension. Her dad was in the middle of planting season and wouldn't get off the tractor. She would have to answer to him later that night. She remembers her brother talking to her on the way home and wishing he could help her deal with things that he couldn't figure out.

"Abbey, what in the hell happened today? I'm sorry that Dad and us haven't been able to be more understanding of what you've been goin' through. I mean with mom dyin', it's been the shits, and I know it; we all do. We just want to help you but don't know how, honest."

"I get it, Billy. The least the little shit could have done was ask me if he could kiss me, ya know? I might not have acted the way I did."

"From what I heard; the poor kid didn't have a chance to ask to kiss you before you dropped him like a sack of beans. Jeez."

"Maybe I did jump the gun. He's a decent kid."

"God damn, Abbey, and you gotta quit swearin' so much. It's not very mannerly, know what I mean?"

"Well shit, Billy, are you hearin' yourself? I mean, that's how we talk. What the eff?"

"Don't say it. I do know one thing for sure, Abbey."

"Yeah, and what's that Billy?"

"I don't think that boy is gonna invite you to prom."

They both had a laugh at that one. It had been too long since Billy and Abbey had had any kind of conversation. They were both enjoying themselves, reminiscing about how much they missed their mom. She had been the glue that kept order in the family and made each day special for all of them.

They talked the rest of the way home, and Billy promised to tell his dad a different version. The suspension would be something else to explain, but they could get their story straight before they got home.

Abbey would remember every single piece of this story and how Billy came to her rescue with their father.

Middle school and high school were not as contentious with other schoolmates. Abbey had little time for the drama that seemed like an everyday event around her, whether it be just walking down the hall, in the cafeteria, or even in the ladies' room. It seemed like it never ended, and each day it would start all over again.

Farm life was a reality check. Get up early, feed the livestock, do your chores before school, and if you had any energy left at the end of the day, play a sport. Abbey was a very good athlete: basketball, softball, and track were where she excelled.

In college, Abbey focused on her academic interests, finance and accounting. Numbers made sense and were not open to interpretation. She didn't have to do the touchy-feely classes that made no sense to her. Abbey graduated in three years with high honors. Her journey to Blue Ridge Vista was odd, but she was glad to be where she thought she could make a difference in the lives of people her mother's age—kinda like the Knights.

Sal was spending the better part of his day working on another project. He thought he would be able to finish it by Thursday.

T had a lengthy conversation with one of his former associates, who confirmed his suspicions regarding EverStar and one of EverStar's operatives within the Kaufman Law Firm. These guys had patiently played the long game, knowing that EverStar had to have the right political alignment as well as cabinet insiders to pull this off. Their plan was working, and they were just waiting to make their announcement.

Buddy asked to get a copy of the deed and title. He made it a business practice to make paper copies of everything. He was old school, preferring paper to electronic files. He wasn't organized, and his desk looked like a bomb had hit it, but once he read something, he remembered it in detail.

The deed was an interesting read. That parcel was in fact dated to 1730, with handwritten descriptions in old English script along with multiple additions. The Adams family had in fact owned the property, and the date on the hearthstone was real, or at least he thought so. Buddy and T agreed that it didn't make any difference whether it was the John Adams family property—historical preservationists would bring national attention to any attempt to sell this land for a commercial and residential real estate development project, regardless of who owned it. Once they knew the story behind it, historians and the media would be like locusts feeding on a cornfield.

Ben had decided to have lunch at the pavilion and happened to see his friend Esther. Ben asked if she would like to join him if she didn't have any plans. She was more than happy to have Ben's company for lunch. It would give them both some time to catch up on the progress they had made. Ben stressed the utmost confidentiality of the information he was about to share, not providing all the details. After all, Esther had provided some financial insight into what the Knights should be looking for to confirm their suspicions on how the department expenses could be a pathway to investigate the fraud. She had been right, and Ben acknowledged her instincts and thanked her again.

As they were talking, De-Lo walked out the E Suite doors and saw Ben. He walked over to say hello. Ben stood up to greet him. "De-Lo, I would like you to meet my friend Esther," Ben said.

"How do you, Esther? I'm De-Lo," he said, then kinda whispered out loud, "I'm Ben's friend; he just doesn't tell many people." And he smiled.

Ben let out his deep laugh, gave De-Lo a hug, and asked him to join them.

"I'd love to, but I have a project I'm working on and just came out to grab a bite to take back to my cubicle. Thank you very much, though. It was nice meeting you, Esther. Have a nice day. See you later, Ben."

Esther was impressed by De-Lo's gentle manner and humor and told Ben as much. She was curious about how they knew each other. Ben said it was a long story, and Esther said she didn't mind hearing about De-Lo and Ben's friendship.

They sat down, and Ben told how De-Lo came to Blue Ridge Vista after being involved in a burglary gone bad.

"Shots were fired. De-Lo saved his friend's life by getting him to a hospital. The police were able to ID De-Lo and his friend easily. He and his friend were arrested. After the arrest, De-Lo's friend told the judge that De-Lo didn't know anything about the gun. The judge placed De-Lo under the supervision of a parole officer and Ruiz, the maintenance super here at Blue Ridge Vista. De-Lo has a monitor on him, and if he screws up, he goes to county jail. Sal and I met him a short time after he arrived, and we just hit it off. He's a good young man who's had a very tough life. He's quite the funny guy. Truth be known, we like having him around."

"I can understand why," said Esther.

Esther said she found Ben's recent news and events very exciting. "How and when are you going to pull off your plan?" she asked.

Ben told Esther that they had figured out the how, but the timing was a work in progress. He explained that there was going to be a dress rehearsal by some of the EverStar team, and they were trying to confirm the date.

"We think the preliminary event is two weeks out, and we have some details we are working through now. It's going to be an interesting story, that's for sure," he said.

Esther was eager to hear more.

Ben promised that he would keep her informed right up to the day before the people from EverStar arrived, whenever that was.

After lunch, Ben thanked Esther again. He enjoyed her company. She enjoyed it just as much, if not more.

On his way back home, Ben decided to swing by Sal's. Without knocking, he walked in. "How the heck are you doing, Sal?" Ben asked.

"In here," Sal answered. "Come take a look." Sal was finishing his project with some tung oil to bring out the grain, just like the others.

"Here you go. What do you think?" he asked.

Ben was speechless, for once. He held the small wooden sword in his hands, admiring the craftsmanship and smallest details.

"It's gorgeous. It looks just like the others. This will mean so much. You did a great job."

"Well thank you, friend, but the real beauty will come after you work your magic. Can't wait to see it."

"Why don't we put it in a different drawer for our next meeting and wait till everyone is sitting, and then you can give it to him then? Sound OK?"

"Sounds perfect to me. I would be more than glad to give it to De-Lo."

"Well then, it's decided."

Ben told Sal that he thought De-Lo being a part of the Knights was a good thing. After all, they needed a younger person to carry on what they had started. Who better than De-Lo? He had a stake in Blue Ridge Vista and would provide some sense of continuity when they were gone.

Ben continued to admire Sal's work, promising he wouldn't screw it up. Sal laughed as he gave Ben a hug. "You're the best, Ben. I mean it."

Ben wrapped the sword in a towel and told Sal that he would have it back to him by Sunday for his inspection. Sal laughed again.

"Oh, by the way, I met Abbey yesterday," Ben said.

Sal, staring directly at Ben, said, "Well, how'd it go? What'd you think?"

"I think she likes you, Sal."

Sal's jaw dropped, and he laughed like he hadn't in years. Ben watched as tears streamed down Sal's face.

"You got me; you got me good, Ben."

Now it was Ben's turn to join in with Sal as they laughed together.

"I think Abbey could really help us a lot. She's abrupt and rough around the edges but honest and understands what the heck is going on at Blue Ridge Vista. I think she's trying to connect the dots like we are. If we share what we found in the orchard, I think she would be all in with our plan. She's smart and a looker, just like you said. We need to talk with Buddy and T because they need to know what we learned from Abbey. We've gotta have her on our team."

De-Lo's day had proven much better for intel results. He casually mentioned to his supervisor, Erica, that while he was getting a cup of coffee, he had heard someone in the E Suite talking about a visit from an investor group. He asked Erica if she knew what they were talking about.

"Yeah, there is a group of young guys coming to Blue Ridge Vista to check us out in advance of the big muckety-mucks who will be here in two weeks.

"The big guys are going to make a major announcement in four weeks about a huge plan for Blue Ridge Vista. I heard through some of the folks here that it will be a major media and political event. Not sure what to make of it, but the guys that own this place have truckloads of money, big money."

"Man, sounds like there's going to be a big party," De-Lo said.

"For sure," she said. "Can't wait. Hope it's good news for me, maybe a promotion. I could use some good news out of this place. It's like there's a whole other plan that nobody knows anything about. I like working at Blue Ridge Vista and the people I work with, at least most of them."

"I hope it's going to be really good news for you, Erica," De-Lo said.

"I heard Abbey say that some big gun from EverStar they call Fitz is going to be coming to Blue Ridge Vista to check us out. Word is he's a real asshole—excuse me, I mean jerk.

Anyway, there are so many stories about the SOB that anybody who gets in his way is gone. I hope Abbey is going to be ready for him." Said Erica.

"Abbey is pretty street smart; she'll figure him out and probably tell him where to get off."

They both had a laugh on that one.

De-Lo would now be able to tell the guys the dates for both the preliminary rehearsal and the major announcement.

Chapter Twenty-Six:

THE FINAL PUZZLE PIECES

T had asked for and received copies of the deeds and titles for the parcel for the old orchard. His friend at the firm had them delivered to him on Wednesday. It confirmed everything T had said about the Virginia Homestead Protection Act, protecting original colonial settlements, passed by the Virginia Legislature. Buddy realized what T had known that he didn't.

It would have been next to impossible to sell that parcel without legal intervention, the kind that EverStar had paid to avoid, and paid a lot. Now that the closing documents were sealed, no one would know, and EverStar could execute their plan. Or at least they thought so.

T had copies of the deeds and titles from Buddy's file, which were not to be shared. The pieces were in order, the video was complete, and De-Lo was working on the final technical elements for the presentation.

Sal was finishing the food prep for the meeting, remembering what Ben had told him about the item for De-Lo. He was preparing more than normal since De-Lo would be attending, and he was smiling as he worked, thinking tonight would be the best meeting ever for the Knights.

Buddy was first to arrive, going directly to the drawer in the living room to get the swords and place them in front of each of the chairs, except one. Whoever was first to arrive always got the swords out of the drawer and placed them on Sal's round kitchen table. The only difference tonight: there were five chairs and four swords.

T was next to arrive, walking in without knocking, and De-Lo was right behind. They greeted each other, said hello to the others, and walked into the kitchen, where Sal had the table set with food and glasses. He had opened a couple of bottles of wine.

Ben walked in last. "Is it Mangiamo time?" he asked.

Sal couldn't resist laughing like always. "You would be correct, Mr. Schein," he said. "Nice to see you, De-Lo," Ben said, "and I think I speak for all of us."

"You are correct," they answered in unison.

They all sat down, Ben reaching for a piece of cheese. "Oh, excuse me. I almost forgot something." He stood up, walked into the living room, and returned with a towel wrapped around something.

Ben stood next to De-Lo and said, "On behalf of the Knights, we would like to present you with this."

He handed De-Lo a sword just like theirs, with a beautiful emerald and a gold band with his initials monogrammed on it, just like theirs.

De-Lo was completely speechless. "I don't know what to say, guys. Thank you all; thank you so much."

"You are most welcome," Sal said. "Glad to have you as the newest member of the Knights. We need someone young like you."

"I would like to propose a toast," said Sal. "To the newest, and by far youngest, Knight." They all stood.

"We are glad to have you join us on our journey to get the guys who are trying to drive Blue Ridge Vista into bankruptcy," Sal said.

"To De-Lo!" They all held their glasses up. "Salud."

De-Lo thanked them again as he passed his sword around for them all to see. It looked exactly like theirs. He covered his eyes, not wanting them to see him cry. Each of them took turns touching his shoulder and congratulating him. He was overwhelmed, staring blankly at his sword, imagining what had just happened, and mesmerized by the experience.

"Now, mangiamo," said Sal. "We have a lot to talk about." They all agreed.

Sal asked De-Lo to start.

He confirmed the dates for the rehearsal. "Great job, De-Lo," they all said.

"Was it hard to find out that information?" asked T.

"Not as hard as I thought it would be," De-Lo said. "Erica, who I am working with, said she heard some of the other folks talking about it. She said they were trying to keep it quiet so that the EverStar people wouldn't draw any attention to their visit before the EverStar owners arrived. Some guy they call Fitz is going to be the lead EverStar guy. Word is he's a real ball buster. This is some big shit they are planning, according to her. Pardon my French," he said.

"That's OK, De-Lo, not to worry. This is big shit they are planning, and we're planning some big shit too, the kind that's going to kick 'em right in the nuts," said T.

None of them had ever heard T talk like that. He was calm and collected and spoke in a matter-of-fact way.

His professional litigation skills told him that the Knights might not have every bit of evidence they needed. However, they had more than enough to embarrass the crap out of the EverStar

Group in front of a huge media setting. Their plan, along with the Knights' help, would fail in a most embarrassing way.

More than ever, T was convinced that the research of the deed and titles, combined with the corrupt practice of his firm, was enough to make EverStar a pariah. It would be hard to imagine that any sponsor or company would want any part of the Blue Ridge Vista project. It would also have a further-reaching impact on the way EverStar would be viewed by Wall Street, which was something they never thought possible. After all, they had covered all their bases, or at least they thought so.

Could there be anything the Knights were overlooking? Was it possible that EverStar had another plan? What if they were wrong? What would happen to Blue Ridge Vista? What would happen to them? What if EverStar had plausible answers?

There were so many questions, but the obvious was just too glaring. EverStar was going to bulldoze a historic landmark to build a premier residential community and a championship golf course on the 850-acre tract and sell Blue Ridge Vista. The pieces were falling into place for the Knights to completely disrupt their plans for both.

The Knights were convinced that EverStar's financial and political gamble was about to explode right before their eyes.

Now, the Knights had a dress rehearsal of their own to do. During the rest of the evening, they shared some thoughts on how to play their hand.

Two options were on the table: Do they give a sneak peek to the junior members of EverStar? They could tease them to get the attention of the owners to talk with the Knights before the big event.

Or do they wait for the big day and let the shoe drop in front of everyone? This would be more dramatic and not give EverStar any cover. It was riskier by far.

T said that they could prepare a media handout for the day of the main event, outlining all their investigative work. They would name names and outline their theory. This would have the most damaging effect on EverStar's reputation, their politicians, their investors, the news media, and the corporations who would be attending.

The discussion came down to what was best for the rest of the Blue Ridge Vista residents, who had no idea what was planned for them.

The Knights might have been too close to all that they learned. Their lives would certainly be affected, just like everyone else who lived at Blue Ridge Vista. But there was more, and it was personal for T and Buddy. They were both honest about what they wanted to see happen to EverStar and the EverStar operatives. The payback was going to be a bitch, and they relished the thought of looking those guys in the eye, in front of everyone, when they delivered the news. It was hard not to make it personal, and T and Buddy were completely open with Sal, Ben, and De-Lo.

De-Lo said he probably should not vote because he was a new member, to which they replied, "Once you're in, you're in." Besides, if he had any interest in staying at Blue Ridge Vista after they were gone, he needed to be there for them. His progress had not gone unnoticed by Ruiz and especially Judge Carmichael, who had connections to help De-Lo if he wanted the judge's help. De-Lo liked Blue Ridge Vista. His grandma gave him a connection to the place as well, and he was glad.

The only thing left to do was to vote.

T asked for them to vote by pushing their swords to the middle of the table as the options were presented. They each looked around the table, smiling at the work they had done to get this far. T reiterated how proud he was of them and what they had accomplished.

Each of them nodded in agreement.

"Now, to the vote. Option one?" They all looked around the table again, sitting still, no emotion.

"Option two?"

One at a time, each of them slid their sword to the middle of the table while T looked around and saw that it was unanimous.

"Now let's get those bastards."

It was decided. The shit would hit the fan on the big day.

There was a request for another meeting before their next round table to talk about the logistics for their plan. They all thought it would be a great idea. They agreed to meet again, this time for dinner on Thursday.

"I'm going to prepare an Italian feast for you guys—bring your best appetites. Capiche?" Sal said.

Ben said, "I'll be here first, but in case I'm not for some reason, don't eat all the food.

Capiche?"

They all laughed, and De-Lo smiled at how these old guys could have such a good time just being in each other's company.

They all said their good nights, or as Sal said, *buona note*. Ben liked the sound of that more.

As he was leaving, Sal tapped De-Lo on the shoulder and asked if he could talk with him. "Sure," said De-Lo. "Sup, Sal?"

"I need to run an errand in town tomorrow, and I am going to need some help lifting something into the back of the truck. Think you could help me? We'd only be gone about an hour."

"Sure, let me check with my boss. I think she'll be fine with it, but I can work through my lunch to make it up if not. I'd be glad to help you."

"Thank you so much. I'll meet you at the main entrance at about ten a.m., OK?"

"See you then," said De-Lo. "Have a good night—I mean, buona note." Sal smiled. "Buona note to you too, De-Lo."

Chapter Twenty-Seven:

GETTING THE PERFECT GIFT

S al was right on time to pick up De-Lo.

"Good morning," Sal said as De-Lo was getting in his truck. "Was everything OK with your boss?"

"Yes, it was," he answered. "She even told me not to worry about making up the time.

She said I have been helping her with all the reports she has been doing lately, so she told me to take as much time as I needed."

"Great," said Sal, feeling a little guilty about not telling De-Lo the real reason he wanted him to come along. He was going to ease into it while they were driving.

They were having fun during the drive, De-Lo sharing how much he enjoyed the round table the night before, especially his sword. It was such a special gift, something he would cherish for the rest of his life. He told Sal how he connected with the other guys; he was truly moved by their acceptance of him into their circle.

Sal explained how much they all felt the same, how proud they were of his progress and the way he lit up their time together. It was also making a difference in the way they were pursuing this whole EverStar thing. De-Lo was going to be the conduit for the Knights and what they wanted to accomplish for themselves and the residents of Blue Ridge Vista. If anyone had questions, De-Lo understood the circumstances of the Knights and his friendship with them. He would be up to speed on everything they were doing and had done. In the event something happened to them, he would have all the information needed to share with Judge Carmichael.

They had not reached out to him yet because they wanted to make sure they were ready for the big day.

At the right time, Sal was going to ask T to contact the judge and explain what the Knights were doing and how they had included De-Lo in the process. They wanted to invite Judge Carmichael to the event as a witness.

T wasn't sure that Judge Carmichael would want to place himself in a position to be a part of the event. He was going to think about that for a while and share his thoughts with the other Knights.

They had discussed quite a lot in a short amount of time when Sal decided to tell De-Lo the truth about why he asked him to go with him today.

"De-Lo, there's something I need to tell you," Sal said.

"Uh oh," said De-Lo. "You're not pregnant, are you?" he said. "No, I don't think so," Sal replied, not missing a beat.

"I wasn't completely honest with you when I asked you to come with me today to help get something in the back of my truck."

"OK…" said De-Lo, not looking at Sal. "What'd you have in mind?"

"Well, honestly, I do need your help, but it's not to lift something into the back of the truck."

"OK, Sal, you're killin' me here. What is it you need me to do?"

"Would you say we're good friends?" Sal asked.

"Yeah, I would, good friends," De-Lo replied. "Good. I'm glad you feel that way. I know I do."

"Sal, where's this going?"

"Well, you see, it's like this." And Sal told him the whole Abbey story, not leaving out any of the details. It took Sal about fifteen minutes to share the entire episode. Ben, he explained, had had the same type of encounter with her.

"Abbey has been under a lot of pressure. She's doing the work of at least two of the executives, who are front guys for the company EverStar has in place. We want to do something nice for her, OK?"

De-Lo looked at Sal and tilted his head a bit. "How does this involve me?"

"Well, it doesn't really involve you directly, but I was thinking how you could help me and Ben."

"I'm still not tracking with you, Sal. Is Ben a part of this caper?"

"What do you mean, De-Lo?"

"You know what I mean, Sal. This isn't my first rodeo. I can see you twitchin' a bit.

Something's up that you ain't telling me the whole deal here, friend—what is it?"

"OK, OK, well, I was hoping, since we're good friends, that you could do me a favor.

It'll be easy for you."

"How easy?" De-Lo countered. "Keep going."

Then Sal handed De-Lo an envelope with the name Tiara on it.

"All you need to do is go into that store and hand that note to Tiara. I've already called her, and she's expecting you. Piece of cake; what do you say?"

De-Lo looked directly at Sal, "Man, you gotta be kiddin' me, Sal. Why me?"

"I just think it would be easier for you, you bein'a young guy and all. Does that make sense?"

"Hell no," he replied. "That doesn't make any sense. Those people are gonna think I'm gay or something. That's not easier for me. A woman's lingerie store? Jeez, Sal, you been takin' drugs or something?"

"It'd mean a lot to me if you could do that," Sal said. "Bet it would," De-Lo answered.

"I'd just feel too uncomfortable—you know, asking a sales-clerk to show me some samples and stuff. Besides, they'd prob-ably like talking to a young, handsome man. What'd you think?"

"I think you must have been hit in the head or something," De-Lo said.

"Look, I won't ask you for another favor, just this little one. I'll make it up to you."

"How ya gonna do that Holmes?" De-Lo asked.

"Oh, I'll think of something, promise. What do ya say?"

"I got an idea," said De-Lo. "Since we're good friends and all."

"What's that?" said Sal.

"How about we flip a coin? That way we can enjoy our friend-ship together, everything being equal and all. Know what I mean?"

"You're a sly one," said Sal. "I'd feel better if you'd do this."

"Like I said, I bet you would. But that ain't happenin' today, and you can take that to the bank. I'll flip you, though, and I know I'll feel better about that. Sound fair to you?"

"I guess so," said Sal. "I just know you'd be better."

"Call it in the air," said De-Lo.

"Tails," said Sal.

As the coin hit the back of De-Lo's hand, he peeked.

"Well, I got good news. You win," said De-Lo. "Yes," said Sal. "It's heads," said De-Lo.

"I thought you said I won," said Sal.

"You did. You get to go in there and describe to the salesclerk exactly what you want, in detail. How's that?"

"No good," said Sal as he opened the door. "I'm gonna feel funny doing this. Are you sure you don't want to?"

"It's all yours. Enjoy it. You might get some ideas while you're in there," De-Lo said.

After about fifteen minutes, Sal came out, looking over his shoulder and around to see if anyone might have recognized him. De-Lo wished he could have been in the store to watch and listen. It would have been priceless.

"Well, how'd it go? Find what you were looking for? Where is it? I want to see it," De-Lo asked.

"I'm having it delivered tomorrow. I need you to do me a favor," said Sal. "They promised delivery at ten a.m.; let me know if you see or hear anything, OK?"

"What the heck did you do, Sal?" he asked.

"Nothing much, just a gift for that special person," he said.

Sal had felt awkward as he walked out of the shop. He had never been in a store like that and was amazed at the different gifts—a whole new adventure. It was something he would share with the guys at the next meeting. He thanked De-Lo for going with him, even though Sal had to be the one to go into the store and buy the gift, but it was done. That was all that mattered at this point.

The drive back to Blue Ridge Vista was more relaxing than Sal thought it would be. He shared more of his family's story with De-Lo, about how his parents made their way to the greatest country in the world and about his childhood. De-Lo listened intently, seemingly captivated.

Sal asked De-Lo if he liked Italian food, because Thursday night was going to be a homemade feast, according to Sal.

"Make sure you come hungry. It's an order, got it?" he said, smiling the whole time. "I can't wait," said De-Lo. "I'm not going to eat lunch on Thursday. Hope you have enough food."

Sal looked at De-Lo in disbelief. "Enough food? You'll see."

They arrived back at Blue Ridge Vista a little after 11:00 a.m. Sal dropped De-Lo off and told him to have a good day. He was going to his place to start on the food. He hadn't completely decided on the menu, but he had a pretty good idea.

On his way back to his place, Sal thought he would swing by Ben's and share the good news. After all, Ben was included in the gift. Sal had felt really awkward in the store, but he wanted to make sure they did something special for Abbey, who had helped them so much. Sal admired her style: blunt, to the point, and never at a loss for words—all character traits that fit her well.

Ben was glad that Sal had decided to do something special for Abbey, and he even wished he had thought of it. No matter—it was done. Sal gave him the heads-up about the special delivery tomorrow morning. De-Lo was on the inside and would be able to share all the details and provide the commentary.

They were both looking forward to the morning and Abbey's surprise.

Once back at his home, Sal started on the pasta, linguine, and spaghetti. He had all the ingredients and didn't need a recipe. He thought he could almost do it blindfolded.

He got out his old hand-crank pasta maker. All he would have to do was change the heads. While the pasta was in the fridge, he started on the meatballs of sausage and ground beef. The sausage would provide the fat needed for the flavor. He also added coarsely chopped onion and celery, minced garlic, basil, oregano, parsley, Italian breadcrumbs, four eggs, and a cup each of Romano and parmesan cheese and mixed it thoroughly. The key to the meatballs was to not try to make them too tight or too large. That was the way his noni had taught his mother.

He would make the pasta tonight and spread it on a towel and gently sprinkle some flour over the top. By morning, it would be perfect. Then he would put it in the fridge. He would also finish the meatballs in the morning.

He planned for a total of three pounds of pasta, half for the linguine and clam sauce and the rest for the spaghetti and meatballs. His kitchen would smell so good. He had four bottles of wine as well. He had a few things left to do, and then he was going to bed, looking forward to the morning.

Thursday was a beautiful day at Blue Ridge Vista. Sal had coffee on his patio and heard Ben announce himself.

"Out here," Sal said. "Get some coffee and join me."

This was what Sal liked the most about Blue Ridge Vista, next to his friends: a moment to enjoy the natural setting—the birds were singing, the sprinklers were on, the fragrance of lilacs was in the air. There were some deer through the clearing enjoying the same morning peacefulness.

"Man, I slept well. How about you, Sal?" Ben asked.

"I slept great, Ben. It's gonna be a great day. I can just tell. I'm counting down to ten a.m. and the fireworks in the E Suite."

"I asked De-Lo to keep us posted if he hears anything."

At 10:00 a.m. promptly on Thursday, a special courier driver arrived at the main entrance to Blue Ridge Vista. No one bothered to pay attention as the driver walked into the main corridor and,

right on cue, said, "Special delivery for Abbey Connors, personal signature required."

A beautiful bag with balloons was in his hands. "Is Abbey Connors here, please?"

The receptionist attempting to hold the delivery man for a moment requested five minutes to get Abbey. It was such a beautiful gift package with balloons.

"I'll be right back," she said as she ran through the doors in the E Hall.

In less than five minutes, Abbey walked into the reception area, looked the guy squarely in the face, noticing the beautiful balloons, and asked, "Are you sure this is for me?"

"I'm quite certain, ma'am. Just tryin' to do my job."

"Wait here. I'll be right back," Abbey said, and she went back to her office to get a five-dollar bill for a tip, returned, and signed the receipt.

Gesturing to the delivery guy, Abbey said, "Here, thank you." The delivery guy smiled and said the same to Abbey.

There was a crowd in the lobby now, wanting to know more about the gift.

Abbey, not wanting to answer any questions, said she didn't know who it was from but would share after she looked at the gift.

She walked back to her office and set the package on her desk. She opened the gift box and looked inside the beautiful gift bag.

Abbey was speechless, which didn't happen often. Her face grew to a vibrant red, and she made sure no one was able to see her gift. She read the card inside the bag:

"We have never done this before, but you deserve something special, just for yourself.

We guessed and hoped we got it right. Your admirers."

People were trying to make their way into Abbey's office to see what was in the bag. She was so embarrassed and thought, *What a nice gesture.* She was at a loss to figure it out, but for now, she just put the contents back in the gift bag, still blushing. She really liked the gift, and it was the right size. How could they have known?

De-Lo, in his cubicle, looked at Erica. "My God, what happened?" Erica asked De-Lo to wait as she walked into Abbey's office. "Abbey, are you OK? What can I do?"

"I'm fine—a bit confused, but OK." She was still red and blushing. "Must have been a very special gift, I'm guessing," said Erica.

"You might say that," she replied. "Yes, you could definitely say that." Abbey left her office, the gift and card on her desk.

Erica looked in the bag, read the card, and felt her face turn a shade of red. She placed the bag on Abbey's chair and left her office.

News travels fast in these workplaces, and no one stuck around to ask Abbey any questions.

De-Lo heard more than he cared to. He was confused. *What in the heck did my new old friends do?* Sal must have really bought something special for Abbey, based on what he heard from Erica, even though she didn't say what was in the bag.

The rest of the afternoon, everyone was abuzz with gossip about Abbey's gift. Abbey was not the easiest person to talk to, by her own admission. She was type A all the way and not one for small talk.

The answers about the gift would have to wait until dinner, hopefully. This had not been a typical day in the E Suite at Blue Ridge Vista, for sure. De-Lo was in the middle of gathering the department reports and other information for Erica so that she could finalize the executive summary for James, Michael, and

Abbey. He would be working until five o'clock for sure, but he would still have time to get cleaned up before going to Sal's.

It was almost six o'clock when the guys started to arrive at Sal's. It was a beautiful evening, not a cloud in the sky. There was a gentle breeze. The view from Sal's home was relaxing, which was a good thing given what had happened today, as De-Lo was about to share. Sal, Ben, T, and Buddy were sitting on the patio before dinner, enjoying the quiet.

"We're on the patio," said Sal. "Make yourself at home. There's beer in the fridge, and the wine is open on the counter."

De-Lo walked out the sliding glass doors to the patio. "How was your day?" they asked.

De-Lo smiled in a different way. "Well, let me tell you, and thanks for asking." Ben said, "I heard there was some commotion in the E Suite today. Is that true?"

"Commotion? Well, you might say so," said De-Lo, looking squarely at Sal. "What happened?" they all asked.

"Well, you see, Abbey Connors, the assistant director of Blue Ridge Vista, got a package this morning from some admirers."

"And?" they asked.

"Well, from what I heard, it took her breath away. I mean, she was as red as an apple. She smiled in an unusual way, according to Erica, and left the office. Erica said the gift was very personal. That's all I know. Maybe I'll hear more tomorrow."

"Wow, sounds like it must have been a neat gift," Sal commented. "What the hell did you do, Sal?"

"What do you mean, What did I do?" he asked.

"You know what I mean," said De-Lo. "What was in the bag, Sal?"

"Just a gift from me and Ben. We thought Abbey could use something nice for having to put up with James and Michael. Besides, we could really use her help, so we thought it would be a nice gesture."

"Whoa, wait a minute, Sal. What do you mean 'we'?" asked Ben. "I didn't know anything about this gift—not that I don't think Abbey deserves something nice for working with those two jerks—but what did you buy?"

"I don't know," said Sal.

"What do you mean you don't know? How is that possible?" De-Lo said. "Well, when you wouldn't go into the store, I had to," Sal said. "It's your fault."

"My fault?" said De-Lo. "How's that?"

"If you had gone in, I wouldn't have; that's how."

"That makes absolutely no sense," said De-Lo, with Ben agreeing.

"Anyway, I went into the store." Sal shrugged as if pleading for understanding.

"OK," said De-Lo. "Then what?"

"Well, I talked to the saleslady and told her about Abbey, described her, and what Ben wanted to get her."

"What I wanted to get her?" said Ben.

"Well, you and me," said Sal.

"So the lady said, 'I have just the right thing. She'll love it; I promise.'"

"Keep going," said De-Lo.

"Yeah, keep going," said Ben.

"Well, that's it—end of story," said Sal.

"What do you mean, 'end of story'?" De-Lo and Ben asked. "What was in the bag?"

"I don't know, really. I never asked. She promised to have it beautifully wrapped and delivered; that's it."

"Sal, so you're telling us you bought a gift but don't know what it was? Really?"

"Yes, really. That's the truth. I thought it would be better not to know."

"Can you believe this? Who would do something like this?"

De-Lo, not missing a beat, said, "Only Sal would even think of something like this."

"Well, thank you," said Sal.

"It wasn't a compliment," said De-Lo, with Ben nodding.

"I love you, Sal, and you're a great guy, but some of the stuff you do…well, it's different, very different. Know what I mean?" said Ben.

"Not to worry," said Sal. "It's done. Hope she likes it, whatever it is. Anyway, it's time to eat."

Sal had enjoyed preparing the food: antipasto, wine—the works. Just a real good Italian meal to share with his friends. That would take their minds off everything for now.

Chapter Twenty-Eight:

ROUND TABLE VI

S al prepared the plates by the stove, which made serving the hot food much easier. He had bowls and plates. Silverware was already set. Wine glasses and water were on the table. The aroma was more intense on the stove. The wine bottles were already open, and Sal placed those on the table too.

"Mangiamo!" Sal said.

Ben was ready; they all were. They were having some casual conversation while in line, talking about the day and what they needed to talk about at dinner. There was a lot to discuss.

Sal was in his element, preparing each plate, making sure they got enough of each different option. It was reminiscent of the meals his mom had made as a kid, and for a moment he paused.

"You OK, Sal?" asked Buddy.

"I'm just fine; thanks for asking. Before I met you guys, I hadn't enjoyed a meal like this with people I like for a long time. Thanks for coming."

"It looks fantastic," said Ben.

"Hope you enjoy it. Now let's eat. If you don't mind, I would like to say grace."

"That would be perfect," De-Lo said, speaking for the rest of them.

They sat down at the table, and Sal asked that they join hands.

"Bless us, O Lord, and these thy gifts, which we are about to receive from thy bounty through Christ our Lord. In Nomini Patri, Spiritu Santi, Amen."

"Amen," they all joined in. "Now, Mangiamo!"

"So how was everyone's day?" T asked.

De-Lo looked straight at Sal, as did Ben. They all shook their heads.

"OK, we heard bits and pieces about something Ben and Sal did today, but not all of it,"

said T.

"You'd better ask Sal," said Ben.

"You'd better ask De-Lo; he was there," said Sal.

"OK already. Can somebody please tell Buddy and me?" said T.

"De-Lo, would you mind sharing so that Buddy and I can enjoy what I think we missed today?"

De-Lo paused. "Well, there was an event at E Suite today that got a lot of attention, to say the least."

"What kind of event? Anything related to the EverStar folks?" asked T, Buddy looking at

De-Lo.

"Not exactly," he answered.

"OK, what was it?" asked Buddy, as he took another bite of the linguine and clams. "This is good, Sal. I've never had this before. I just love it."

"Thank you very much," said Sal. "I'm glad you enjoy it."

"I'm enjoying everything tonight," Buddy replied. "Well, what about the event today?" he said, looking at De-Lo.

De-Lo decided to take a drink of wine. "The wine is good, Sal. Excellent nose." They all looked at De-Lo.

"What did you say?" asked Buddy. "Excellent nose?"

"You been hanging around us too much, De-Lo," said Ben. "Sal has turned you into a real wine snob."

"I don't mind you guys makin' fun. I just needed to see if you were payin' attention." He laughed out loud.

Now they all were looking straight at De-Lo to finish the story. "C'mon," T said. "We need to hear this story."

And with that, over the next ten minutes, De-Lo shared the entire story, not leaving out any detail. He began with the trip to the store to make the purchase and concluded with Abbey's reaction in the E Suite.

Erica was able to confirm to De-Lo that Abbey's gift was a silk robe. Abbey loved the gift but wanted to know the gift givers.

T and Buddy were speechless, just staring as Ben and Sal continued to eat. De-Lo reached for the wine bottle.

"OK," said Sal. "Who wants some more pasta? There's plenty of both linguine and spaghetti. Please get some more."

"I'm not bashful," said Ben as he pushed his chair back. "This never gets old. Thanks again, Sal."

T tilted his head to his right side, looking at De-Lo, then toward Ben and then Sal. "Well, I guess I'm glad I asked about the gift," said Buddy, shaking his head in a slow and deliberate manner. He wondered what Abbey would do and how it might affect what they had planned, and he said the same to them all.

"I think she'll be fine," Sal said casually.

"Oh, you do, do you?" said Buddy. "What makes you think so?"

"Well, if that just happened to me, I wouldn't want anybody to know. I'd just accept the gift and wonder who was kind enough to give it to me," said T.

"But you don't know who gave it to you—that'd make me crazy," said Buddy.

"I think we're fine. She'll wonder who was so thoughtful," said Sal as he and Ben kept eating, both having another glass of wine.

"C'mon, we're good. Now eat some food. I'll be glad to warm it for you guys," said Sal.

T and Buddy reached for their wine. When they finished their glasses, they poured some more. They were enjoying the company and the food more than the recap of what sounded like a very weird day, to say the least.

"Next time I ask how your day was, just don't tell me, promise?" said Buddy.

T and Buddy decided to get more food as well, enjoying everything Sal had prepared, still trying to absorb what they'd just heard.

They still needed to discuss their plan for the main event, which was four weeks away. T thought that the Knights needed to have a backup plan, which he shared over dinner. "Let me explain my thinking, if you don't mind," he said. "We need to assume that EverStar will have security to prevent any disruption of their announcement. After all, they have a ton of money they have already spent. Some old guys with a hunch aren't going to spoil this for them."

De-Lo was working on the technical side, preparing the video of the orchard and the hearthstone to make it more dramatic. The trick would be timing it to preempt EverStar's presentation. He had talked with T about creating a lighting disturbance manually. Buddy agreed to help on what he called his "technical expertise", which really meant turning the lights off at the right time. They all thought it was simple enough to work. De-Lo would give Buddy the cue.

T had a rough draft of a concise media handout. He had bullet points to draw attention to all the different parties involved. EverStar would lead the way: names of the congressmen on EverStar's payroll and the secretary of transportation—who not only received funds from EverStar but had also directed some $200 million of unspent COVID-19 funds to help support and fast-track the road project—the corporate sponsors for the planned golf tournament, and EverStar-owned environmental, social, and corporate governance interests that would have major construction contracts.

There was more to add, but T hoped a one-pager would get the media attention he wanted.

T asked for questions. "Please tell me what you think. We need to get as much as possible out in the open."

"I have a question," Sal said. "Is the stuff EverStar doing legal?"

"Yes," said T. "It borders on corruption of government officials and misuse of public funds, but the media is on their side."

"Well, how do we win?" asked Sal.

"Yeah," said Ben. "If this is legal, what's the point of all our work? I'm not trying to be negative, but can we stop them?"

T explained the different approaches to getting the attention of EverStar and the media. If T was right, exposing the Adams property was their best bet. They needed the media to carry the water for them and to question EverStar about their motives and interests. If the media was able to push EverStar, their corporate connections and tournament sponsors—Titleist, Callaway, TaylorMade, FedEx, and ESPN—would get cold feet. It would be bad for their business and their reputation.

These facts, combined with how EverStar had gained their information with the help of the Kaufman Law Firm, showed that what EverStar had done was illegal. T had the proof, hoping it wouldn't come to that, but he was prepared to expose it.

"After all of my talking, I'm hungry," said T.

"That's a good thing," said Sal. "We have plenty of food; get some more. I must tell you, T and De-Lo, I'm impressed with what you guys have done. This is like something you would read about in the newspaper. The thought that this EverStar bunch can do this kind of stuff with the help of the government and politicians makes me sick."

"What do you think?" asked Ben. "I know these guys screwed with you, and I'm sorry for you, Buddy."

"You're right, Ben, they did screw with me, and my partner screwed my wife, so I got it twice. I want to watch T drop the hammer on these guys. That will make it all worth it for me."

De-Lo shared the video he had prepared. He wanted T to do the commentary because of his knowledge of the Virginia Homestead Law, which would place the whole project in jeopardy.

T wanted to prepare a narration to track with the video. They could do that tomorrow. For now, they'd had a full day and a great meal.

"De-Lo, could you come by my place tomorrow after work so we can get this done?"

"Sure can," he said. "I can be there by five thirty, OK?"

"Great. Now I want to finish my food. This is so good, Sal."

They all stuck around, talking and eating and drinking a little more. It was nice in so many ways. They could all use a break from their work. The remainder of the week would be relaxing, or so they thought.

De-Lo was more tired than he thought.

"If you guys will excuse me, I'm heading back to my room. I need some rest. You all have pretty good endurance for old guys," he said, laughing. "See you tomorrow."

"Good night, De-Lo," they all said. "Be safe and make sure you go straight home. We don't want to worry about you, OK?"

"I got it, Ben. Straight home, like I'm gonna go out clubbin' or somethin' at the BRV lounge."

After De-Lo left, Sal said, "There's something I wanted to talk to you guys about if you don't mind."

Ben returned to the table, sat down, and said, "OK what's up, Sal?"

"This is a little awkward for me, but I was thinking that De-Lo doesn't have anyone but us. I mean, with his grandma gone, he's got no family."

"What are you getting at, Sal?" asked Buddy.

"Well, I was thinking, if there's any way we could give or leave him some money when we're gone, it would be a nice thing, know what I mean?"

"That's nice," said T. "It sure would make things a little easier for him when we're gone.

I know I would be more than glad to help him financially in some way." They all nodded. "Yeah, great idea, Sal."

"Thanks for listening," Sal said.

They discussed it further as they all helped clean up dinner. Ben selectively reviewed the cannoli tray one more time before choosing the chocolate.

In less than an hour, Sal had packaged leftovers for each of them to have the next day.

Tupperware was an amazing invention.

"Good night, you guys, and sleep well," Sal said.

Chapter Twenty-Nine:

The Laughter Is Gone

Tuesday morning was as beautiful as Sal could ever remember at Blue Ridge Vista. The sprinklers, the birds, the sun—just perfect. He had placed the leftover cannoli on the counter in anticipation of Ben's arrival. They would make an excellent morning treat to go along with their coffee. He couldn't wait for Ben to see what he had prepared.

It was 7:15 a.m., and his friend would be there any minute. Sal checked the coffeepot again; he knew Ben liked the espresso with a little cream.

By 7:45, Sal was a little on edge, so he decided to walk over to Ben's home. Like Sal, Ben had placed a key under a pot on the front of his entryway so any of the guys could come in when they wanted. Sal knocked first just in case Ben was in the shower. He waited a bit longer, got the key, and opened the front door. Ben was relaxing in his favorite chair, looking out on the beautiful Blue Ridge Vista property.

"Ben, what's up, buddy? You OK? I was waiting for you to have coffee. I was going to surprise you with some cannoli for breakfast."

Sal walked over and tapped him on the shoulder. "Ben."

Sal paused, and he nudged Ben a little harder, thinking he'd just dozed off for a brief nap.

Sal shook Ben harder, still with no response, and his worst fear was confirmed. His dear friend had passed away. He didn't know when but thought it must have been sometime earlier in the morning, as he was dressed in his usual gray Sansabelt slacks, white polyester shirt, and Velcro slip-on shoes.

Sal checked his neck for any signs of breathing and tried to get a pulse, but there was nothing, nothing he could do.

Sal sat down beside Ben, reached for and held his hand, and cried. Sal shook with the pain of a broken heart for his dear friend. Sal looked around and saw an envelope addressed to De-Lo.

Sal called T and Buddy to let them know about their friend. They were at Ben's front door in minutes, each pausing in disbelief. They had all been together just last night, enjoying what they had accomplished and still had planned. They shared a moment of reflection for their friend, each touching his shoulder and smiling at how he had made them all more sensitive and appreciative of his generosity.

"What do we do?" asked Sal. "Should we call the main office, ask for the executive director?"

"I'll call the executive director," T said. "In the meantime, let's look around to see if we can find any family contacts, OK?"

"Sounds good," said Buddy as Sal handed T the envelope with De-Lo's name on it.

"I found this next to Ben's chair when I came in. I want to make sure we give it to him before anyone gets here, OK?"

"Sure. Why don't you keep it with you, and we can give it to De-Lo, T said. "Gladly," said Sal.

It wasn't ten minutes before there was a knock at Ben's door. "Anyone here? I'm here from the Blue Ridge Vista management team."

T opened the door. "What can I do for you?" It was Abbey Connors.

"Our dear friend has died," Sal said, tears streaming down his face. "Abbey, thank you so much for coming."

Abbey gently tapped him on his shoulder, "Not to worry, Sal. I want to help you and your friend Ben, OK?"

"Absolutely," Sal replied.

"Do any of you know of his immediate family?"

"Unfortunately, we do not," T responded.

"Why don't you look around, and I will have our office review his entry documents to see what we can learn. I'll contact our health services office so they can make the proper arrangements, OK?"

"Thank you, Abbey; that would be great," Sal said.

T said, "We need to call De-Lo. Buddy, would you mind giving him a call? Ask him to stop by Ben's if he could, OK?"

"Sure," said Buddy.

"Abbey, could you please let us know if we can do anything? We feel helpless, and we appreciate what you are doing for our friend. Thank you," said Sal. "I mean it from the bottom of my heart."

"I believe you, Sal," she said.

Just then, there was a knock at the door. De-Lo walked in. "What's up, old guys? Where's Ben?"

Sal walked over to De-Lo, gently touching his shoulder. "We have some sad news, De-Lo. Ben has passed away."

De-Lo stood in shock. "Don't mess with me, guys. That shit ain't funny."

T said, "I'm sorry, De-Lo. Sal is telling the truth. He went by Ben's place earlier when Ben didn't show up for his morning coffee. When he came in, he saw Ben resting quietly in his chair. Sal tried to wake him, but our friend had already passed."

De-Lo turned his head as tears filled his eyes, embarrassed at his own pain. "It's OK, De-Lo. We all loved Ben and know how much you loved him too."

"I'm tired of this shit," De-Lo said. "My grandma, my friend Ben—this shit has got to stop. What are we going to do now?"

"Abbey is helping us figure that out now," said Sal.

De-Lo sat down in the chair next to Ben, touching his hand, and quietly said something to him as though expecting Ben to respond.

"You were nice to me the first time I met you," De-Lo said. "You never judged me, always encouraged me. Thank you."

Each of them shared words of comfort, and each of them felt the same pain. Their dear friend who had the special laugh and smile looked like he was resting comfortably because he was. They all felt the pain as they tried to console one another, remembering Ben's kindness.

Abbey was in complete control, making calls and arrangements, directing the Blue Ridge Vista facilities services.

She had been right when she told Sal that she was the real director of Blue Ridge Vista. By her calm demeanor, she proved that and much more as they all watched and listened.

After Abbey finished her call, she told all of them what Blue Ridge Vista would be able to do and then asked what they would like done for their friend Ben.

They looked at one another and asked if they could think about it and let her know later in the day. For now, they wanted to see if they could try to find any of Ben's family to notify them.

Abbey would be working on that too and assured them she would keep them informed on anything she learned.

"I am going to leave you now. Here's my cell phone number. Please call me or text me with any questions. The ambulance will be here shortly."

"Thank you, Abbey. We appreciate everything you are doing for our friend," said T. They all nodded, tears still in their eyes.

They sat down at Ben's kitchen table, wondering what they were going to do. They all felt alone, each of their own lives a story of loneliness, but they had one another, and that they knew.

"I remember the first time I met Ben at Blue Ridge Vista; he made me laugh and smile.

He was just a wonderful person," said Sal.

"I heard his laugh before I met him," said Buddy. "You couldn't not be attracted to him."

"I remember when you told me that you were going to call me T. Ben laughed because he

said my name was too long. I didn't say anything because I liked it."

Sal, still crying and laughing, remembering their conversations and stories, was taking deep breaths. "He was like nobody else I have ever known. 'You don't have to tell me "Mangiamo" twice.' I can still hear him saying that as we would have dinner. What a beautiful person."

"I remember his glasses, the nose piece with the tape, his clothes, his style—everything about him. I never knew anyone like him," De-Lo said. "When I got my sword, the work you and Ben did, all of you to make me feel welcome. I just thought, 'These guys are old, but they're cool,'" De-Lo said as he smiled.

"How are we going to honor Ben?" De-Lo asked. "I mean, we have to do something special for him. He did so much for us."

They looked at one another, thinking that De-Lo had spoken for all of them. "We need to come up with a great idea, don't we?"

"You are right, De-Lo. We will come up with a great idea to honor Ben," said Buddy. "Yes, we will."

They all knew their meetings wouldn't be the same without Ben, but they still had a lot to do. The first thing was to make sure all the arrangements for him were going to be perfect.

Abbey would take the lead, and they would follow.

There was a knock at the door; the ambulance team had arrived. The medics were especially kind and respectful.

"We are going to take Mr. Schein to the health-care facility as required by law. There are some reports and documents they need to complete. They will notify Abbey, and she can let you know what happens beyond that. So sorry for your loss."

"Thank you, guys," they all said. "Please be careful with our friend."

"We certainly will," they responded.

After Ben was gone, they sat down, trying to regain their composure. There was a lot to do.

"You think Blue Ridge Vista would let us have a memorial service for Ben here?" asked Sal.

"I wouldn't see why not," said Buddy. "Why don't we ask Abbey?"

"I think Ben would like that," said T.

"I agree," said De-Lo. "I think Esther and others would like that very much."

"Would you guys like to come by for coffee, and we can talk more?" asked Sal. "Sure," said T and Buddy.

"I need to get back to work and check in with my supervisor," said De-Lo. "I'll check back with you guys later."

"Before you go, when we got to Ben's, there was an envelope with your name on it beside his chair. This is for you from Ben," said T.

"What is it?" asked De-Lo.

"I don't know," said T. 'You'll have to find out."

De-Lo put the envelope in his pocket and wiped the tears from his eyes. T gently placed his hand on De-Lo's shoulder. "Ben liked you a lot and I know you know that." De-Lo cried some more, turning away from T.

They looked around to see if there was anything they needed to do at Ben's before leaving. Sal thought they should make sure his home was locked before they left.

"What do you think we should do with his keys?" he asked.

"Why don't we put them in a different place that we know will be safe?" said Buddy. "Good idea," said T. "That way if there is anything we think of, we can come back and get it," T said, not knowing what that would be.

The walk to Sal's was like a bad dream. No one said anything, but they all knew they were thinking the same thing. What were they going to do without their dear friend Ben?

Sal opened his door and walked by the drawer in the living room where the swords were. He opened the drawer, reached for Ben's sword, walked into the kitchen, and placed it in front of the chair where Ben had sat.

Sal poured out the coffee and asked if anyone wanted something else to drink.

It was past noon now, and T said, "You know, I'd go for a beer if you have one."

"Me too," said Buddy.

"I'll have one too," said Sal, pausing to remember how Ben's laughter would lighten up the entire room.

"You know, it was awfully nice of Abbey to take control of things for Ben and us," said

T. "She had a calming presence the whole time."

"She absolutely did," said Sal. "I'm glad we did something nice for her."

"I want to know what you guys are thinking," asked T. "What should we be doing now?"

"Since Abbey is looking for some of Ben's family, why don't we talk about what we are

going to do and say for his memorial. He was such a special friend to us. I remember when I first saw our swords after Sal made them. Out of nowhere, Ben made the gold bands with our initials and inset our birthstones. Who does something like that?"

"Ben does," said Sal. "He was amazing in so many ways. I smile just thinking of him. Boy, I couldn't believe how much he could eat. I knew he loved our time together just as much as we loved him and the joy he brought to us."

"All the more reason that we need to honor him by completing our work on EverStar," said T.

"You know, I was thinking, what if we bring Abbey into our circle and tell her what we have been working on? I mean, she probably would have a real interest in what we are doing, and she'd be perfect to confirm what we suspect about the financial management at Blue Ridge Vista. We show her the video, and T explains the Virginia Homestead stuff and what happened at his firm. Buddy can explain how he got robbed of a big commission. What do you think?" asked Sal.

"You know, it couldn't hurt. I think if what you said about Abbey and how she feels about James and Michael is true, then she could help us and help herself," said T.

"Sounds like a plan to me," said Buddy. "Why don't we wait until after Ben's service to talk with her? I think we should include De-Lo in the conversation because he has a lot at stake as well, OK?"

"It's decided," said T.

They sat around for the better part of the day, sharing Ben stories, laughing, crying, and wishing it all were a bad dream.

De-Lo's walk back to his office was a bit slower than normal. He decided to open the envelope that Ben had left for him. He read the handwritten note:

> *You have made me smile in a cool way. Every time we talk, I enjoy listening. I wanted to leave you a little something to help you out. Hope it fits, that's my joke. So, this is from B…. Now you be D and I be B, what you think of that Holmes?*

Inside was a check for five thousand dollars. De-Lo cried some more.

T decided to call Abbey to see if she was able to locate any of Ben's family and what the arrangements would be.

Sadly, she confirmed, Ben had no immediate family, just the Knights and some of the other people he had met at Blue Ridge Vista. How sad, they thought, and how important it would be for them to make his memorial that much more special.

Abbey was able to make funeral arrangements with a local mortuary. She had also arranged for a large picture of Ben to be placed in the main lobby at Blue Ridge Vista for the next several days. The visitation would be tomorrow, and the graveside service would follow that afternoon. The guys were going to Ben's to pick out something for his viewing and called Abbey to let her know they would bring his clothes by later in the day.

Abbey offered the Blue Ridge Vista van and a driver to take them all to the visitation. She also told them that she had reserved a small room off the main entry if they would like to have a reception for any of their other Blue Ridge Vista friends following the gravesite ceremony. Sal made a special visit to her office to say thank you for all she had done for them, especially Ben.

Tomorrow was going to be a long day. T called De-Lo to let him know what was planned so that he could attend if his supervisor would excuse him. Without pause, De-Lo said he would be at the service and asked if there was anything he needed to do. T mentioned that he might think of something he would like to say at the service because all of them were going to say a few words.

Buddy and T arrived at Sal's at 7:30 a.m. for coffee, each dressed in a suit. Sal had on a sport coat, a tie, and slacks. They paused to look at each other. They cleaned up very well for old guys.

"What do you think Ben would say to us?" T asked, looking at them and wondering the same thing.

Buddy said, "Let's mangiamo."

They just shook their heads. Buddy was right, and they tried not to cry.

In a few minutes, De-Lo showed up, dressed in the clothes that he had worn to his grandma's funeral.

"I think we should be going; I don't want us to be late," T said. "You guys look great; I mean it."

"You're not too bad yourself—for an old guy, I mean," said De-Lo, breaking the ice.

They all just shook their heads as they walked to the front door, Sal reaching into the drawer in the living room.

The walk to the main entrance of Blue Ridge Vista took a little longer this morning, as none of them were in a hurry to say their goodbyes to their friend.

Abbey met them in the foyer, commenting on how good they looked. She explained that the driver would take them to the visitation and the cemetery and stay with them until they returned to Blue Ridge Vista. She was thinking that they would be back around three p.m.

"Call me if there is anything you guys need," she said.

"Abbey, we can't thank you enough for how much you have done for us and our friend Ben," Buddy said, and they all nodded in agreement.

They arrived at the funeral home and were greeted and escorted into the parlor for Ben's visitation. They stood in a line shoulder to shoulder, right by his casket, just staring at Ben and each thinking comforting thoughts. Sal got next to the casket, reached into his jacket for Ben's sword, and placed it carefully in Ben's folded hands. They each touched Ben's hands and spoke quietly to him one last time.

"That was nice," said Buddy. "Now he can rest peacefully."

It was only the four of them at the visitation until Esther arrived. She spoke with each of them, sharing conversations with them about Ben and how much he loved being a member of the Knights.

About thirty minutes later, Abbey arrived. She greeted each one of them and said how sorry she was for their loss. She didn't have to be there, but she was, and they appreciated her taking the time to join them. Abbey was the only Blue Ridge Vista employee, other than De-Lo, who attended Ben's wake.

It was a short drive to the cemetery. Now it was just the four of them as they exited the Blue Ridge Vista van. A person from the cemetery met them and asked them to follow him to the gravesite.

There were two of them on each side of Ben's coffin, and one by one they spoke, expressing they're thanks to the guy who had made them all smile.

De-Lo was the last to share his comments, expressing how his heart was broken for the second time.

"I can tell you that you made a difference in my life," he said as he turned to all of them. "You all have. I never thought for a minute that I would like hangin' with a bunch of old guys, and I mean it. But there's something about you all. You welcomed me; you helped me when you didn't have to. Who does that?" he said, tears welling in his eyes.

T touched De-Lo's shoulder, "Old guys like us do that for good guys like you, OK?"

De-Lo just shook his head, still crying. It was the pain of the loss of Ben and the kindness of all of them that overwhelmed him.

"What do you say if we join hands and say a prayer for our dear friend?" said Sal. "That's a great idea," they all replied.

Sal went first. "Dear Lord, we know our friend Ben is with you now. We pray that you take extra good care of him because he has meant so much to us. He taught us kindness, generosity, and how to laugh and enjoy life. We trust your guidance as we continue the work that Ben has started. Thank you for your grace and mercy. Amen."

"Sal, I don't have anything to add. That was beautiful," said T.

"Neither do I," said Buddy. "Thanks, Sal."

They turned and made their way to the van. The drive back to Blue Ridge Vista was easier than the drive to the cemetery, for sure.

Once they arrived, they walked into the main lobby, where they saw the picture of Ben on an easel. It was a great picture of his gentle smile. Abbey had done so many things for them, and this was just one more.

Sal walked toward her office and knocked gently.

"Excuse me, Abbey. I just want to thank you for everything, all that you have done. It was perfect. I want to invite you to dinner on Monday night at six o'clock at my home. T, Buddy, and De-Lo will be there. We want to share something with you. I hope you can make it."

"I would be glad to accept your invitation. I look forward to joining you all, thank you."

"See you then and thank you again."

Sal and the guys walked back. De-Lo went to his office to finish the day.

Sal told them that he had invited Abbey to their round table on Monday night.

"I hope you don't mind, but I've been thinking that Abbey could really help us. She knows everything about what's going on at Blue Ridge Vista. She is especially aware that James and Michael don't know what's going on. I really believe that she would be motivated to help us."

"Good idea," said T.

"I agree," said Buddy. "Anything she can add will be helpful. Glad you asked her."

Sal was relieved that he hadn't overstepped his bounds with his friends. He wanted all the help he could get, and he was convinced that Abbey knew a lot about EverStar that the Knights didn't.

Chapter Thirty:

THE NEW KNIGHT

Sal worked on the dinner menu. There would be the usual antipasto that they, especially Ben, had enjoyed. Dinner would start with an arugula salad with sliced almonds and light olive oil dressing with a balsamic glaze. The main course would be penne pasta with marinara sauce and a side of veal. Dessert would be biscotti with a limoncello chaser.

The guys arrived a little early, feeling awkward reaching into the drawer in Sal's living room for their swords. They sat at the table, no one wanting to talk first.

Sal broke the ice. "I'd like to propose a toast to our friend Ben. Could you please join me and stand? To Ben, who made our time together here at Blue RidgeVista so much more enjoyable and meaningful. We will finish our work. Salud." They all touched glasses. "To Ben."

There was a knock at the door. "Please come in," T said.

Abbey made her way into the living room. "Nice place you got here, Sal."

"Thank you very much, Abbey. Glad you could make it."

"I am as well. Thank you, guys."

"Please join us. Can we offer you something to drink? We have beer, wine, a cocktail if you prefer?"

"A Scotch and water if you have it would be fine," she said. "Please have a seat," said De-Lo.

Abbey asked, "De-Lo, how'd you get hooked up with these guys?"

"You mean these old guys?" he replied, laughing. "It's a long story but a good one. I'll tell you sometime when we can talk longer. I think these old guys have something they want to tell you."

"OK," Abbey said. "I'm all ears."

Sal started to serve dinner. "You don't mind if we eat while we talk, do you?"

"Not at all," Abbey answered.

T began their story and theory, not leaving out any detail. Abbey listened intently, taking mental notes and nodding in agreement as each new detail made the picture come together in a more complete way. She was amazed at how they had pieced this all together without the benefit of confirming the financial details. She had been completely unaware of the Homestead Land component of the story, but the EverStar urgency to start the project now made more sense.

Abbey had been doing some additional investigation into this Fitz guy, and his EverStar reputation was unbelievable. She had figured out that he was getting copied on an email stream from James and Michael. He was also aware of all the financial mess that they had created and was the reason that James and Michael were not worried at all about anything they did. Fitz had their backs, at least they thought so. Abbey shared this with the guys.

"That's amazing," said Buddy. "These guys are lowlifes."

"Wow, T and Buddy, I'm sorry for what these guys put you both through. I understand your passion to drop the hammer on them," said Abbey.

"You know, Abbey, EverStar has that major announcement in less than two weeks. We are asking for your help with what we are trying to do. We think there are going to be some big fish that are going to be caught up in some serious legal and criminal shit, if you pardon my language. What do you think?" asked T.

"I think we can confirm enough of the financial wrongdoing to go with what you all have uncovered to make a lot of people look bad—I mean *bad*. Their plan to set up two LLCs, one for the eight-hundred-and-fifty-acre tract of land and one for the Blue Ridge Vista Senior Living Center, makes complete sense. EverStar can bring in a third party to drive Blue Ridge Vista into the ground. I think that process has already started, based on the financials."

"We'd like you to see the video that we have from the old orchard on the southeast part of the Blue Ridge Vista property, OK?"

"Sure."

De-Lo handed his phone to Abbey to view the location and the hearthstone.

"Oh my God," Abbey exclaimed, a chill coming over her. "Those guys knew this and were going to sweep it under the rug during the construction of the new development?"

"We are almost certain they knew, based on the number of attorneys that EverStar has on staff. Had it not been for Sal and Ben trying to fit through the debris, we never would have known. But once we did, we figured their guys had read all the deeds and titles and were suspicious enough that they should have disclosed this to the EverStar executive team."

"We think that they had so much invested politically and financially that they couldn't back out. I mean, this is an eight-hundred-million-dollar deal, at least. They are going to be paying a lot of people in their food chain," T said. "Sound reasonable to you? Because I did the math on the golf course and development in some rough numbers to get a sense of the magnitude of the project.

An average golf course is taking up about one hundred and sixty to one hundred and eighty acres. This one will be nearer two hundred acres, to fit more building sites around the golf course, which will sell for more. That leaves six hundred and fifty acres, less seven to eight percent for infrastructure. Let's say the lots are one acre each, at a minimum. They will easily get three hundred lots around the golf course at one million dollars per lot; that's three hundred million dollars. They have another six hundred–plus acres at seven hundred thousand dollars to eight hundred thousand dollars each. Split the difference. That's another three hundred and sixty million. That doesn't include golf course memberships at a hundred thousand dollars each, limited to three hundred members. Tack on another thirty million dollars, plus security for the gated community, other built-in charges for this exclusive place only twenty-five minutes from Washington, DC. And that's in terms of today's dollars. It will be easily ten to fifteen percent more when the bypass is under construction. EverStar will presell half of this and cash flow the entire project. When you consider EverStar bought this out of bankruptcy for about fifteen million dollars, you can see how they operate, and that doesn't include the ten acres that Blue Ridge Vista sits on. What a sweetheart deal they made."

They all listened to T's description of the math and the unbelievable amount of money that EverStar was going to make, unless they could stop it.

"Now I can see why this is such big shit," Abbey said. "Sorry about that. This is going to be a major news event as well, people from all over: senators, representatives, EverStar guys flying in. Wow."

"We could use your help, if you would help us," said T.

After listening to all that, Sal interrupted. "Who would like something to eat or another drink? We've been working up an appetite. I know I could use some more food and another glass of wine. "How about you, Abbey? I know these guys aren't bashful."

"You know, I'd go for another bit of veal and a glass of wine," Abbey said. "Great choice," said Sal, and he fixed another plate.

The other guys just helped themselves.

"Abbey, we could use your help coordinating a video of the old home in the orchard," said Buddy. "I know De-Lo has made the video but getting some audio and visual help would make this thing come to life in a way they won't like."

"It sure will," said T.

"Does anyone else at Blue Ridge Vista know what you have done here?" asked Abbey. "No, only you," said Sal. "That's why we wanted to share this with you—because we know that you are the one who makes this place work. We trust you."

"Well, thank you very much. I appreciate your trust," she said. "I can get De-Lo all the help with the video piece. Blue Ridge Vista has an excellent system in place, and it will come to life when we're finished with it, promise. We can get this done tomorrow. Is there anything else you need?" Abbey asked.

"Well, to be honest, we don't know what we don't know as far as what will happen after we do this. I mean, we love it here at Blue Ridge Vista. We don't want anything to happen that would cause us or any other residents to move someplace else," said Sal.

They all agreed, even De-Lo.

"You know, when I heard what you old guys were doing, I laughed and said to myself, 'There's no way they can stop this EverStar project.' But the more I listened and watched how much this meant to you, I was all in. Besides, you don't know shit about technology, excuse my French," De-Lo said, and he laughed out loud.

"Really?" asked Sal. "Is that the way you're going to tell the story?"

"OK," said Abbey. "I'll work on confirming the guest list for the event. I know James and Michael keep that stuff hidden. They tell me I'm on a need-to-know basis, a bunch of shit—pardon my French," she said, and she laughed with the rest of them. "I have my ways; it may take me a couple of days, but we'll have it for you."

"That's great; thank you," said Sal. "This means a lot to all of us and the rest of the people here at Blue Ridge Vista who don't know what these jerks are planning. It's going to be great to see how this crumbles all around them."

"Is there anything else you can think of, Abbey, that we should be doing?" asked T. "No, but if I do, I'll let you know. I think we should meet again just to review our plan after I confirm who all will be attending, OK?"

"Perfect," said De-Lo. "I would like a little more pasta, Sal."

"Help yourself, De-Lo. There is more of everything. Mangiamo, in honor of Ben."

The next week was a blur, with the group reviewing all their work, waiting for daily updates from Abbey on the attendees, and trying to help with Ben's home and belongings. They all helped as much as they could.

Sal, Buddy, and T had an idea to do a voice-over on the video. They would ask Abbey her thoughts so she and De-Lo could work that into the presentation. If they were going to use a voice-over, they wanted to make it fact-based and brief.

They also talked about what they expected to happen after they did their presentation.

How would the EverStar people respond? What would the media do? What would the fallout be?

They decided to prepare a media handout for after the video part, but there was going to be a lot of commotion. T was glad that he had shared his idea with Judge Carmichael and that he agreed to attend the event. There was no way of knowing how the EverStar crowd would attack the Knights and Abbey.

Abbey could certainly confirm the way the Blue Ridge Vista financials had changed and the way the monies were moved from one account to another. She would also be able to verify the timing. She had maintained a separate file to document when and how much money was moved to make the financials look better for the EverStar board of directors. She had also established an email chain of concerns with James, Michael, and Fitz dating back to her second month of employment. She just needed to make electronic copies of the emails and copies of the financials in case there were problems with her computer.

She had a thumb drive and a backup, one in her purse and one at her condo. This wasn't her first rodeo. The thing that made Abbey angry the most was that James and Michael didn't think she was smart enough to understand what they were doing. This Fitz guy was part of the mix as well but at a much higher level within EverStar. She told them time after time that if someone ever reviewed their decisions on the Blue Ridge Vista financials, they would be in trouble. They both tried to placate her without answering her questions, and that just made her decision to be a part of the Knights' mission an easy one.

Even though Abbey knew she had more than enough information at this point, she needed to be careful not to overplay her hand. She also needed to make sure that she wouldn't raise any suspicions about her information gathering. She was able to confirm that the CEO of EverStar intended to attend the event. She learned this through Ruiz, who had a friend who worked at the local airport. EverStar's corporate jet had filed flight plans, and Ruiz's friend had confirmed that to him. Five other corporate jets had done the same. This was a very big deal.

Abbey and De-Lo had been able to download the video onto their desktops so they could critique the content. While it was a bit rough, the lighting was excellent given the challenges they had to overcome. A voice-over would be a great addition, done by T, who would confirm the Virginia Homestead Act and the 250-acre parcel that was planned to be consumed for the housing and golf development.

T would calmly cite Virginia law and the work his firm had failed to disclose before the sale. Buddy would provide a brief comment on what happened to his files before EverStar acquired the entire tract. The expeditious closing and the 25 percent offer above the sale price and thirty-day closing were more than incidental to the deal.

With their tremendous wealth and influence, EverStar was able to orchestrate their plan for Blue Ridge Vista. Fitz was going to be the quarterback. Major corporations have public relations firms and consultants for just these types of events: coordinating electronic and print media, reaching out to state and local authorities, and more. EverStar's internal intel and data revealed that the financial impact of their plan for Blue Ridge Vista could easily hit the billion-dollar mark. The land development deal and TV rights from the major networks for the golf tournament would be a seven-figure annuity.

T was finalizing his part and, in the process, decided to go to the Middleburg courthouse to research the original Adams deed. He wanted to confirm what they suspected just in case there were any questions. Sal offered to drive T and talk with him, hoping to learn more about how he could confirm the property ownership. It would be a process to dig through the city and county records. He just wished that Ben could be there with them because he had been such a part of the whole plan.

During the drive, T confided in Sal how much it hurt him to be forced to leave the firm that his father had founded. He never would have thought anything like that was possible. It made him more determined to expose the whole EverStar plan and watch the politicians go down with them.

Sal was a great listener during the forty-five-minute drive. He and T talked about their families, wishing there were things they could do over. Blue Ridge Vista had given them both a new purpose, one they wanted to see to the end, whatever that would look like. What they were doing today would help solidify their plan.

The old Middleburg Virginia courthouse was a thing of beauty, built in the mid-1800s and with gorgeous architectural elements and statues of not only Virginians, but the great leaders of the United States. They agreed that a return trip was in order because they didn't have enough time today to see all the history before them.

The archives were in the basement. T had been online in advance of the trip to save time. The huge ledgers were in a special location with special security. He had emailed in advance to explain what he wanted to review. A person escorted T and Sal to the exact part of the room, and the ledger was retrieved by a person wearing special gloves. T and Sal would have to wear gloves as well while they were touching the pages of the huge leather-bound books. Sal got chills as he watched T delicately turn each page, history staring them both in the eyes.

The county had done an amazing job preserving the history of Virginia and the United States. T and Sal both felt like they could spend days reading through these documents.

T found the pages he was interested in. He used his cell phone to take pictures of the room, the large leather-bound volume, and the picture in the archives. He planned to include this in the video they were preparing.

The history of John Adams was remarkable: a statesman, a philosopher, an ambassador, an American patriot and leader, and a legend who lived to be ninety years old. The Knights had uncovered his original home, which was an incredible story that many would not believe—they barely did themselves—but it was true.

T had all the information and photos he needed. Sal was impressed with the way T was taking notes and sharing with him how the Adams family had settled in this part of Virginia.

T closed the book and thanked the security person for his time. He was asked to leave the volume on the table as they were escorted out of the basement.

During the drive back to Blue Ridge Vista, Sal and T talked about what would happen after the EverStar plan was exposed. They hadn't given that much thought. But they did agree that they would enjoy watching EverStar and all their henchmen try to dig themselves out of the hole that they had created. It would be worth the price of admission to watch EverStar and their attorneys explain how this entire mess happened. How was it possible that EverStar didn't know about the Adams family property? So many questions, so much finger-pointing. They enjoyed the thought together. It was one thing for EverStar to go down in this mess; it was quite another thing for all the other golf corporate sponsors, course designers, media, and celebrities to be attached to the extravaganza that was a bust. Money can only buy so much power and prestige; reputations can be lost when spent on bad relations. EverStar was going to find out how deep their pockets were.

T thought it would be good to check in with Abbey and plan to have a meal for all of them to review the final product. Sal agreed that they could have some pizza at his place. It would give them a chance to critique their work and make any final changes.

"How about six o'clock?" Sal said. "Perfect," said T.

They arrived right on time, early, and they reached into the drawer in the living room and got their swords. Sal asked about drinks.

"I'm in a beer mood tonight," said Abbey.

"We can do that," said Sal. As they all sat down, Sal excused himself. "I'll be right back."

They talked about their day and what they had learned. Abbey confirmed that an EverStar corporate jet had filed flight plans with the local airport. She also learned that five other jets were scheduled to arrive early on the day of the announcement. James and Michael had taken a Zoom call from Fitz and were acting kind of nervous. She was convinced that Fitz had given them a sneak preview of what EverStar was planning. Buddy had the dates and copies of all the reports that had been copied without authorization, and T had his notes and photos of the Adams property deed. They had accomplished a lot.

They all had some pizza and were engaged in conversation when Sal spoke. "Excuse me, I have something I would like to say. When we began this project, we stumbled a bit. I mean, I stumbled, and more than a bit. What I'm trying to say is that with Abbey, we have found an advocate for our cause, and we know we're right. We've got a fight on our hands, and those bastards don't know who they're messing with. Anyway, I would like to present our newest Knight, Abbey, with this token of our appreciation. To Abbey," he said as he handed her a sword with her initials engraved on it.

They all joined in a toast.

"Here's to Abbey," De-Lo said as he stood with the rest of the Knights. "To Abbey, thank you. We couldn't do this without you," said T.

Abbey was overwhelmed and speechless, and she was embarrassed for them to see her tears. They all tapped her on her shoulder gently. "We're proud of you, Abbey," said Sal. "Really proud of you. I don't have Ben's skills; this is the best I could do."

"Thank you; thank you so much," said Abbey, "I don't know what to say."

"You don't need to say anything," said Buddy. "We appreciate all you have done and are doing to help us and the residents of Blue Ridge Vista."

"Why don't we review everything one more time?" said T.

De-Lo played the video with the voice-over. He would add T's photos in the morning.

T handed out a mock-up of the media handout and asked for comments. "I think it's important to keep this concise. I made four bullet points. What do you think? Do we show the video first or do the handout?"

"Good question," said Sal. "I think we play the video, let that set in, and use the handout as a backup—a thought. How about you all?"

"Abbey, you have more experience in the corporate climate stuff. What do you think?" asked T.

"I think we preempt the EverStar intro with the video because we know the media cameras will be going. That's my thought," Abbey said. "The video is powerful and well done. Look."

Abbey and De-Lo had hit a home run. The video was perfect. They would all have handouts for the crowd. Game day was in two days.

They sat around, eating pizza and just having a nice time without stress, wishing Ben were with them.

"Any last-minute thoughts?" asked T.

"Yeah," said De-Lo. "What the hell are we going to do when this is over? I mean, what are we—I mean you old guys—going to do for excitement? I worry about you sometimes."

"Wow, I never expected that," said Sal. "I mean, you worryin' about us old guys…must be your softer side. We just haven't seen it before."

"What the hell, Sal? You guys beat it out of me, turned me into a real easy touch," said De-Lo. "Anyway, what do you think is going to happen after we do this video in front of all the media and EverStar guys, Abbey?"

"Not sure. There's going to be a lot of explaining. I think the media will have a field day with EverStar and the politicians. It will warm my heart, along with James and Michael having to explain how they misappropriated Blue Ridge Vista funds. Yeah, it will be interesting, to say the least. There may be some folks going to jail."

"No kidding," asked De-Lo. "I didn't think of that."

"Yeah," said T. "At a minimum, the project gets halted, and Blue Ridge Vista will be safe. If I could offer some advice, I think it would be wise to put the entire Blue Ridge Vista property, including the Adams property, in a land trust. That would protect it from future schemes like the one that EverStar had planned. I am confident that the Virginia Legislature would be glad to acknowledge all that we have done to protect this historic property."

"What a great idea," said Abbey. "That would be wonderful. It would give the residents and their families peace of mind knowing that they are safe from intrusion and any plans to try to do something like this again."

Chapter Thirty-One:

THE REVEAL

On the morning of the EverStar announcement, the place was all abuzz. Fitz had set up an area for the pros to put on a golf exhibition, with artificial turf placed near the veranda. The pros could hit their drivers down the meadow in the direction of the old orchard. The EverStar video feed had the course designer's rendering of the much-anticipated Virginia course, complete with waterfalls and several lakes. The course designer had flown in to be a part of the media event. He was explaining to the media how his design would take full advantage of the natural beauty of the existing landscape, preserving all the mature trees and gently rolling terrain.

Fitz was schmoozing all the pros and the equipment company's representatives, making sure that they all knew that he had planned the entire event. He was dripping with smugness at what he had done. James and Michael were like lapdogs, following Fitz around and making sure they were no more than three feet away from him at any time during the preannouncement gala.

The Knights had followed the news reports of the incoming bigwigs. Everything was set.

The media arrived early with three DC news stations, including national reporters, and positioned themselves around the Blue Ridge Vista property, trying to get the best lighting for their telecasts.

Titleist, Callaway, TaylorMade, and PXG had their touring buses positioned in plain view for all the media to see, with their sponsored pros on hand for the meet and greet. They were signing autographs and posing for pictures with the Blue Ridge Vista residents and the employees. Fitz had managed to be included in many of the photos. James and Michael even got in a few. They were feeling a bit more cocky than normal. EverStar had spared no expense, paying for all the promo costs. This was truly a huge spectacle. There was a live feed from ESPN, and the Golf Channel was streaming the whole event.

A huge limo made its way up the long Blue Ridge Vista drive. The top three EverStar executives worked their way out to be caught willingly on camera as they waved to the crowd and shook hands with the DC pols. Fitz casually walked up to greet the EverStar execs, gently tapping each on the shoulder, like he was the EverStar CEO. James and Michael were just steps away. This was their first time to see any of these guys. They only had heard their names and seen their faces on Facebook and other social media sites. Smiles were everywhere, for now.

A security firm that was contracted for crowd control escorted the EverStar Group to the main lobby for a brief prepared statement, and then they would take questions. Their presentation had been professionally created by a large media consulting firm. It would tell of all the great things that EverStar had done for their self-serving causes. Greg Norman would do the intro for the golf course, highlighting the signature holes and the work done by the designer to preserve the integrity of the beautiful landscape. It was full of the stuff the media would be drooling all over it. Fitz had orchestrated everything, and he was smiling as the crowd worked their way into the pavilion.

Fitz walked to the front of the room, microphone in hand. He said a few words and then introduced his boss, the CEO of EverStar. There was a quiet tone to his delivery as he thanked those attending and shared his vision for this major development for the golf course and the entire community. He highlighted the financial impact of the EverStar investment in Blue Ridge Vista and how it would benefit the local economy. He also noted that people would thank EverStar for making this commitment and investment.

At that moment the video was interrupted by a "technical issue with the lights" the Knights' video and T's narrative. T was standing next to the old orchard where the Knights had found the remnants of the Adams homestead.

"I would like to welcome you to the original home of the John Adams Family."

There was dead silence as T continued. He started to walk around the area, looking directly into the camera, calmly explaining how the Virginia Homestead Law was passed by legislature to protect lands from commercial and residential development. T explained that the John Adams family home behind him was a piece of history to be protected and preserved. He briefly told how his old firm had acquired some of the original land documents illegally.

The guests looked up in confusion. The media news teams' cameras were rolling. The EverStar CEO apologized for the mix-up. People listened intently as the volume of the sound system increased.

"Excuse this confusion," said the EverStar CEO as he looked for Fitz in the crowd. "I don't know what's going on right now, but we'll have it corrected in a moment."

Fitz was in the back of the pavilion looking for James and Michael as he tried to make his way to stop the video feed in the rear of the ballroom. He was too late to stop anything.

James and Michael scurried about like hamsters, looking at each other in disbelief. They turned to Abbey, and she smiled. "What the hell is going on, Abbey?" they asked.

"The truth," she replied. "I told you assholes what was going on, and you didn't believe me. You just ignored me, but not anymore. You two dicks have a lot of explaining to do. If you'll excuse me, I have an interview to do. Have a nice day, because I'm going to enjoy this."

Fitz found James and Michael. He was in their faces, the veins in his neck bulging as he ripped them up in front of everyone. "I knew you two dickheads were worthless, and you proved it today. Get out of my face and pack your shit up. You're fired. I don't ever want to see you two pieces of shit again."

The EverStar CEO was standing behind Fitz as he was giving James and Michael a verbal beating only to catch his wrath in full frontal form.

"I don't know what the hell you were thinking, but you have cost EverStar for the last time. I don't ever want to see you again. You're fired. These guys are going to escort you off this property. Get out of my face. Don't bother trying to get on our jet. You can take a bus home. A lot of people are going to hear about what you did here today, I promise you. Your family name can't save you."

As they were walking away, Abbey couldn't resist the chance to jam James and Michael. After all they had done to make her time at Blue Ridge Vista a living nightmare, she was at ease.

Abbey walked up to them and paused. They were talking to themselves.

"So, what are you assholes going to do now? You sure tried to screw things up here.

What in the hell were you two dumb shits thinking?" She turned to see Fitz walking toward her.

"I suppose you're the bitch that that caused all the trouble today. I can tell you that I'll make your life a mess. Got it?"

With that, Abbey turned as if to walk away, paused, walked directly toward Fritz, pretended to trip, and bent over. As he looked down to see if she was OK, she kicked him right between the legs with all the force she could. He dropped like a bag of beans, moaning so loud that a gathering formed around him. The security guards helped him to his feet while enjoying his pain.

"You know, you're a real piece of shit. Somebody should have told you that a long time ago, so I'm doin' you a favor. Get out of my face."

Abbey turned and walked away, looking for T, Buddy, or Sal.

She didn't have any idea what was in store for her future, but she really didn't care. She knew she had acted profession-ally—at least up until now, and except for her language, which was a work in progress.

The media had questions for all the EverStar executives, who were trying to find cover from the entire fiasco.

"How could this happen? Did you know that the land was the original John Adams family farm? Did you know the Vir-ginia Homestead Law would not permit your development plans? Who made the decision to develop this historic property into a gated residential golf community?"

The media was questioning the major corporate sponsors who had been introduced before the event. They were trying to make their way to their limos, but the media vans were block-ing the driveway.

It was funny to watch politicians not wanting to be caught on camera. They didn't know where to hide. There were questions for everyone and no real answers. It was a thing of beauty in its own way, to watch as the politicians tried to scurry for cover and avoid being held accountable for their involvement in the entire EverStar mess.

A news reporter made her way to T, as she had spotted him on the video. She asked if he would mind answering a few questions. He asked Abbey to join him.

"If you'll excuse me," said T, "I would like to introduce Abbey Connors, assistant director here at Blue Ridge Vista and the person instrumental in assisting our efforts to expose the EverStar fraud."

With cameras rolling, other news agencies funneled their way toward them. Abbey spoke calmly and provided specifics on how the Blue Ridge Vista execs had misappropriated funds to enhance the balance sheet. When asked how she could prove her claims, she said she had emails and other correspondence that would corroborate it all.

When asked, T provided the backdrop of what happened at his firm. It was a long story, but the media ate it up. There were more questions, and he patiently answered each one, with Buddy at his side. Buddy was able to share more details on the land, specifically how all his work had been given to a third party and then to EverStar.

Sal stood back with De-Lo, watching the hysteria unfold, listening to as much as he could from T and Buddy and thinking how smart they both were.

"Well, what do you think, De-Lo?" Sal asked. "Not bad for a bunch of old guys, you think?"

De-Lo smiled, caught up in all the excitement. "Sal, to tell the truth, if this is what you thought was going to happen, I mean, this is some serious shit."

"You are right, De-Lo, this is some serious shit—a perfect description. I wish Ben were here to enjoy this with us, you know? I would love to hear his laugh one more time."

De-Lo nodded his head in agreement.

"You know, De-Lo, in answer to your question, I had no idea what would happen, but then again, this was my first time being a part of something like this. To tell you the truth, it feels lit, as you would say," said Sal.

"You could certainly say that" De-Lo replied, "This is amazing. I'm loving this confusion. What a day."

Chapter Thirty-Two:

THE BEGINNING

Abbey was holding all the cards. One of the EverStar executives was able to have a brief conversation with her about her future. He assured her that this mess would get cleaned up. It might take a while, but it would be done. In the meantime, he asked if she would assume the CEO position at Blue Ridge Vista. She could choose her own team, and she wouldn't have to deal with James, Michael or Fitz.

He promised a 30 percent salary increase, Abbey said 50, and he agreed, along with an executive benefits package. She would have the employment contract later in the day.

"I hope you will accept this offer. I apologize for what you have had to endure. I want to make sure that EverStar makes this right because our reputation has been badly damaged today, and there are some people who are going to need to get attorneys. I liked the way you handled Fitz, he's quite the asshole, if you know what I mean. It's a long story to explain why he ever worked for EverStar."

"I accept your offer. Thank you very much," said Abbey.

Sal waited for the right moment when he saw the crowd finally give Abbey a break. She was able to have a well-deserved drink of water. He was walking toward her when she saw him.

He shook his head and smiled. They stopped and nodded their heads in agreement, both smiling now and waiting for the other to say something. It was a long pause. They both dropped their hands to their sides.

"Damn it, Sal, say something," Abbey blurted out. "I mean, what the heck? You did it!

We did it! You guys were great. You didn't need this fight, but hell, you got those assholes."

"We did," said Sal. "You were great. Ben and I admire you, we all do. You're an amazingly strong woman, and you deserve the best. You kicked their collective asses."

Sal reached out his hand to shake Abbey's and gently kissed her on the cheek. "Well done, Abbey."

All in all, it had been a good day—a little wild, but good. It was going to get better. Abbey wanted De-Lo to be a part of the new Blue Ridge Vista team, and she could make it happen. His work to expose the whole EverStar mess proved his skills and judgment. He had a great sense of humor and was always willing to learn; he would make a great member of the team. He would keep everyone on their toes with his style and quick wit.

Life was going to be boring in the future. What could the Knights do for an encore? They decided to continue their regular dinner at Sal's, and Abbey would have to come and keep them up to date on the latest happenings at Blue Ridge Vista. She gladly accepted their offer.

Abbey would ask T to be the legal counsel for Blue Ridge Vista. There was still a ton of work to do to untangle the whole mess created by EverStar. They would not merely walk away from all they had invested in the Blue Ridge Vista project. Ever-

Star had serious work to do to mend fences with all the corporate sponsors, the golf equipment companies, the media, and the congressmen who were trying to disassociate themselves from anything EverStar. T would be the perfect Blue Ridge Vista advocate. Besides, T and Sal were going back to the Middleburg, Virginia, courthouse to do a deeper dive into the Adams property. That was a promise they had made to each other, and it would be kept.

Abbey decided to offer Buddy the director of sales job for Blue Ridge Vista for the patio homes. Buddy had shared his vision about expanding the patio homes' footprint. Abbey knew that Buddy was a natural to continue doing what he did best, sell. He convinced Abbey it would easily cashflow the construction costs, and she was all ears because it made perfect financial sense.

Sal was reflective about all that had happened and some things he hadn't thought about for some time. As he walked back slowly to his home, he tried to imagine how things were going to change at BRV, as De-Lo called it.

Sal had promised himself that he would call his cousin whom he hadn't talked with in a while. He had an amazing story to tell him. They had worked together when they were kids and had some great laughs. This was a story he wouldn't believe. Sal was having trouble believing it himself.

Acknowledgments

This story is dedicated to the memory and inspiration of my daughter, Polly, the joy and love of our lives. At an early age, Polly possessed writing skills and an insight into human behavior well beyond her years. She was as beautiful as she was kind. Our family misses her so much but cherishes the time we had together.

To my son, Stephen, and his wife, Darci, and their beautiful sons, Max and Leo. Stephen now understands what we meant when we said, "Wait until you're a parent." He and his beautiful family provide such tremendous joy in our lives every single day.

And to my patient, understanding, loving, and beautiful wife, Claire, an English major and teacher, middle school principal, and elementary school principal, who correctly diagnosed my ADHD long before it was the buzzword in social behavior and education. It was also confirmed by my doctor. Claire knew that even though I was a sociology major, every now and then something interesting and original might surface...just kidding. I love you, Claire.

About the Author

Neil Marchese grew up in Pittsburgh, Pennsylvania. He was the middle of five children to Eugene and Carmen Marchese. Neil graduated from North Hills High School and DePauw University, where he met his wife, Claire.

He has very fond memories of his family and siblings, Kathleen, Eugene, Lynn, and Brigida. He enjoys golf, fishing, and cooking, but most of all the time spent with his beautiful family.